PUFFIN CANADA

THE FALLS

ERIC WALTERS is the highly acclaimed and bestselling author of over fifty novels for children and young adults. His novels have won the Silver Birch Award three times and the Red Maple Award twice, as well as numerous other prizes, including the White Pine, Snow Willow, Tiny Torgi, Ruth Schwartz, and IODE Violet Downey Book Awards, and have received honours from the Canadian Library Association Book Awards, The Children's Book Centre, and UNESCO's international award for Literature in Service of Tolerance.

To find out more about Eric and his novels, or to arrange for him to speak at your school, visit his website at www.ericwalters.net.

The Falls

ERIC WALTERS

PUFFIN
CANADA

PUFFIN CANADA

Published by the Penguin Group

Penguin Group (Canada), 90 Eglinton Avenue East, Suite 700, Toronto,
Ontario, Canada M4P 2Y3 (a division of Pearson Canada Inc.)

Penguin Group (USA) Inc., 375 Hudson Street, New York, New York 10014, U.S.A.
Penguin Books Ltd, 80 Strand, London WC2R 0RL, England
Penguin Ireland, 25 St Stephen's Green, Dublin 2, Ireland (a division of Penguin Books Ltd)
Penguin Group (Australia), 250 Camberwell Road, Camberwell, Victoria 3124, Australia
(a division of Pearson Australia Group Pty Ltd)
Penguin Books India Pvt Ltd, 11 Community Centre, Panchsheel Park, New Delhi – 110 017, India
Penguin Group (NZ), 67 Apollo Drive, Rosedale, North Shore 0632,
Auckland, New Zealand (a division of Pearson New Zealand Ltd)
Penguin Books (South Africa) (Pty) Ltd, 24 Sturdee Avenue, Rosebank,
Johannesburg 2196, South Africa

Penguin Books Ltd, Registered Offices: 80 Strand, London WC2R 0RL, England

First published 2008

1 2 3 4 5 6 7 8 9 10 (WEB)

Copyright © Eric Walters, 2008

Manufactured in Canada.

LIBRARY AND ARCHIVES CANADA CATALOGUING IN PUBLICATION

Walters, Eric, 1957-
The falls / Eric Walters.

ISBN 978-0-14-331246-8

I. Title.
PS8595.A598F34 2008   jC813'.54   C2008-901070-1

Visit the Penguin Group (Canada) website at www.penguin.ca
Special and corporate bulk purchase rates available; please see
www.penguin.ca/corporatesales or call 1-800-810-3104, ext. 477 or 474

The Falls

ERIC WALTERS

A man isn't defined by where *he lives,*

but by how *he lives.*

CHAPTER ONE

I LOOKED DOWN AND SAW the stain on my T-shirt. It looked like dried ketchup. I scraped at it with my thumbnail and flaked away a little bit, but couldn't remove it completely. Damn. I didn't want Candice to think I was a slob. Maybe I'd go home and change my shirt. My house wasn't close, though, and there was no guarantee that anything I had there would be any cleaner. My mom had just started doing the laundry instead of me, but she'd missed last week because she'd been offered an extra shift at the casino. Besides, it really wasn't that big a stain. Maybe Candice wouldn't even notice. Then again, *I'd* noticed.

I started to tuck my shirt into my pants—not all the way, just enough to hide the stain. There, that took care of it.

I took a deep breath. "Hi, I was just in the neighbourhood and . . ." I stopped myself. That didn't sound right. Besides, what if she asked *why* I was in the neighbourhood?

"Hey, Candice, do you remember me from last night at the party? I'm Jay and . . . what am I saying?" I demanded of myself. If she didn't remember me then I was in serious trouble and shouldn't be going there in the first place. But how could she not remember me? It was only the night before . . . or, really, early that morning. She hadn't left the party until almost two, and it wasn't like she was drunk or anything . . . I didn't think she'd had more than two or three beers the whole night.

"Hey, Candice, I was just—"

"Excuse me?"

I practically jumped up in the air as I startled out of my trance. There was an old woman with a grocery buggy standing on the sidewalk right in front of me. I'd been so lost in thought that I hadn't even seen her coming.

"I didn't understand what you were saying," the woman said. "Were you talking to me?"

"I was . . . I was just talking to myself," I stammered.

She nodded her head. "I do that all the time. That and talking to my cats. Cats are such good company, don't you think?"

"Um . . . sure . . . I guess."

She smiled. "Are you lost? Do you need help?"

"I'm okay. Thanks, anyway."

She smiled again. She certainly was a happy old lady. She started tottering away, her little grocery buggy trailing behind her.

Actually, she wasn't that far off when she'd asked if I was lost. I knew where I was, but I certainly was lost in a different way. I probably shouldn't even have been there. I should have just gone home. I'd bump into Candice sooner or later, somewhere around town. It wasn't like Niagara Falls was so big that you could avoid running into people for long. In fact, try as hard as I could, there were always some people I ran into wherever I went and . . . but she wasn't one of them. We went to different schools, and before last night I'd never even seen her before.

And I *knew* she *did* want to see me—she'd talked to me a lot at the party, and come over to say goodbye before she left, and told me she was happy to meet me, and even told me where she lived. That had to be more than just being polite. You told somebody where you lived because you wanted them to drop in sometime. It had to be that. Definitely. Well, almost definitely.

I looked up at the house. That was the right address. That was her house. There were cement steps leading up from the sidewalk to her walkway. I took the four steps in one bound. It was a long walkway and the grass on both sides was worn and beaten down. The flower bed by the porch was untended and filled with weeds. I stopped again, this time at the stairs leading up to the wooden porch that wrapped itself around the front of the house. There were a couple of missing spindles, and peeling paint. It held some lawn chairs, a bike—maybe it was Candice's bike—and a broken-down old couch.

The house was big, and brick, and tall. When it was built—maybe seventy or eighty years ago—it was probably pretty fancy. Now it just looked faded and tired and in need of repairs and a good paint job—like most of the houses in town. A lot of them weren't even houses anymore, really. They had been subdivided into apartments. On a lot of the houses there were three or even more doorbells at the front door, each leading to a different apartment—one in the basement, maybe two on the main floor, another on the second floor, and sometimes even a tiny one in the attic up on the third floor. It was amazing how many people—how many *groups* of people—could be crammed into one house.

Me and my mom had our whole house to ourselves. It was the house she'd grown up in, her parents' house . . . until they died. My mom was thinking that maybe it would make sense for us to rent out the basement. That wouldn't be so bad, and the rent money couldn't hurt. Money was always tight. Besides, it would be different having somebody living in our basement than it had been for us to live in somebody else's basement. Over the years we'd lived in a couple of basements, and I never wanted to do that again. I hoped we'd never *need* to do that again.

I climbed the stairs, the second and third steps sagging under my weight. I looked at my reflection in the glass of the front door. My hair looked wild. It stuck up and out in twenty different directions . . . not in a good way. I ran my fingers through it, trying to straighten it out or flatten it down or something. That didn't seem to be working, and I couldn't very well tuck my head into my pants like my shirt. It would have to do.

"Hi, Candice . . . Hello, Candice . . ." I said softly, rehearsing my opening line just one more time.

I raised my hand to knock and the door swung open. A man—balding, heavy-set, his belly hanging out from under his shirt and overflowing over the belt of his pants—stood in the doorway, scowling at me. I took a half-step back.

"Yeah?" he barked.

"Does Candice live here?" I asked meekly.

"Who wants to know?" he demanded.

"Me. Jay . . . Jayson Hunter."

"Hunter," he said, and smirked.

"Is this where she lives?"

"I'm her father."

"Is she home?"

"Yeah, she's here, but you can't see her," he said, his smirk changing into a scowl.

"Is she busy?"

"She's always going to be too busy to see *you*," he said.

"I don't understand."

"What don't you understand? You can't see her."

"But I just wanted to—"

"I know *exactly* what you wanted and it ain't happening, *buddy boy!*" He'd leaned in closer as he spat out the last few words, and I could smell alcohol. It was still only ten-thirty in the morning. Either he'd already been drinking or he'd had so much last night it was oozing out of his pores.

"My Candy doesn't have any time to waste on a loser like you!" he barked.

I felt my spine stiffen and a flush run over my body. "I'm not a loser!" I protested.

He laughed. It was a loud, raspy sound that was filled with bitterness. "The fruit doesn't fall far from the tree, buddy boy."

"What?"

"You ain't never heard that expression before? It means you're a loser like your old man was a loser."

"My old man? You don't know anything about my father."

"I know who you are," he said. "I know who your family is, *Hunter*. I went to school with your old man."

My father's last name wasn't Hunter, and besides, this guy looked way too old to be the same age as my father . . . the age he would have been if he were alive.

"I remember your old man racing around town, thinking he was somebody 'cause he had some beat-up old Harley and a leather jacket! I remember. And I remember him knocking up your mother—she was hardly older than my Candy is now—and then not being man enough to stick around and—"

"Shut up, you fat old fart!"

His face froze mid-sentence. He took a step toward me but I didn't budge an inch. My fingers curled up into fists. He was bigger than me, but I knew I could get in a couple of licks before he hit me. I might even be able to pop him, and he'd be so stunned that I'd dance away before he could lay one on me . . . it wasn't like he'd be able to catch me once I got a few feet away.

"Beat it!" he yelled as he reached out and poked me in the chest with a finger.

I brushed his hand away.

"You want a piece of me?" he bellowed. His breath was a foul combination of alcohol, cigarettes, and stale food, all mixed in with the smell of sweat coming off his clothes and body. I backed away a step to get away from the terrible odour.

"I'm through being nice!" he screamed.

Through? I hadn't seen any "nice" so far. He suddenly spun around and fled through the door, leaving it wide open behind him. What was he doing? A tingle went up my spine. He wouldn't just leave and—

"I'm gonna break you up good!" he screamed as he charged through the door again, swinging a baseball bat in front of him!

I put a hand on the top of the railing and leaped off the porch, clearing the flower bed and landing on the grass, tumbling over and rolling. I looked back in time to see the bat slam down on the railing—right where I had been standing!

"You wanna chase after my little girl, do you?" he screamed. "Let's see how fast you can run with two broken legs!"

I scrambled to my feet and ran off his property, jumping down to the sidewalk before I stopped. I was safe there.

"I ever see your face around here again and this bat is gonna do all the talking for me!" he screamed. He slammed the bat down against the top of the railing again and one of the spindles shattered!

I cringed.

"Beat it, you loser!"

"Look who's talking!" I yelled back. "You want to see a loser, look in the mirror sometime . . . that is, if it doesn't crack!"

"Come on up and say that, you little coward!"

"I'm not the one who had to go and get a baseball bat because he wasn't brave enough to face me without one!" I yelled back at him. "You were too chicken to face me man to man!"

His expression changed from anger to outrage and he got all red in the face. He dropped the bat to the floor of the porch and started lumbering down the stairs.

I didn't want to fight him, with or without the bat. He was fat but he was also big. I crossed the road and started down the street.

"Running is probably the first smart thing you ever did in your whole life . . . loser!" he bellowed.

I turned around and gave him the finger, but I kept moving.

He kept yelling—the same thing, over and over. His voice got fainter and fainter until I turned the corner and his words were gone completely. I could still hear him inside my head, though—the same words echoing around and around and around.

"You're a loser . . . a loser!"

CHAPTER TWO

I TURNED ONTO CLIFTON HILL. The neon signs hadn't even been turned on yet, but the road was already jammed with cars packed with tourists, people who'd come from all over to see Niagara Falls, one of the Seven Wonders of the World. At least that's what it said on the postcards and T-shirts. I didn't even know what the other six were but I figured the Falls had to be number seven on the list.

I could sort of understand that people might want to see it, but living here you soon realized that it was nothing more than some water falling over some rocks and kicking up a bunch of mist. Nothing worth driving hours and hours, much less *days*, to see. They'd all crowd around at the railing, *ooh*-ing and *aah*-ing at the sight and the sound and the mist, all excited. Well, all excited for a few minutes. After that it was just more of the same. So after taking a few pictures they had to figure out what they were going to do next. They'd spend the rest of their time—and

money—going to the House of Horrors, or the
IMAX theatre, or the Guinness World Records
Museum, or eating in one of the hundreds of restau-
rants, or maybe gambling at the casino.

Some of the locals didn't like the tourists crowding
everywhere. Some of the tourists could be really
annoying, but I knew we had to be grateful. If the Falls
didn't attract them—and then bore them—people
like my mother wouldn't have jobs. She was a blackjack dealer at the casino. So I guess those tourists put
food on our table and a roof over our heads. I knew
that—and I knew what it was like to have neither. We
lived here because those people, those tourists, just
kept on coming, day after day, week after week,
month after month, year after year . . . to see some
water falling over some rocks.

Carefully I crossed the street, threading my way
through the traffic, watching out for those drivers
who were too busy looking around trying to see the
Falls to watch where they were going. I cut down an
alley that led me away from the bustle of the business
district and onto my street.

The traffic sound faded away but I could still hear
a faint roar—the sound of the Falls. There was no place
in town you could go to escape that sound. I read once
where a long time ago, the winter was so cold that
a massive ice dam choked off the river and no water
could get through—so the Falls stopped falling. It was

the middle of the night but the sound—or I guess really the lack of sound, the silence—woke people up. And they got out of their beds and left their houses and went and stared at the rocks, the place where the Falls *was*, but *wasn't*. Finally, after hours, while everybody in the entire town stood there watching, the water broke through the ice and rushed down the dry riverbed and roared over the Falls. Man, even I would have driven days and days to see *that* happen.

I walked down the long driveway of a house. I had to go to the back door—the door that led into the part of the house that my friend Timmy and his father lived in. I knocked on the door and listened. There was no answer. I knocked louder. Even though it was almost eleven I was sure I was waking him up. He didn't need to sleep any more. I started to pound on the door and—

"Keep your shirt on!" I heard a voice yell from behind the door. It opened up. It was Timmy. "Hey, Jay, man . . . what are you doing here?"

"What do you think I'm doing?" I asked. "I'm here to see you."

"You woke me up, man," Timmy said, as he stretched and rubbed his eyes.

"You're already dressed," I pointed out.

"I went to sleep in my clothes," he said. "It saves a lot of time in the morning. So, why are you pounding on my door so early?"

"Early? It's practically noon," I said, smudging the truth by an hour or so. "Come on and I'll buy you breakfast."

"Breakfast?" Timmy asked, and he perked up. "Like bacon and eggs?"

"Like a coffee and a donut at the Donut Hole."

"Even better. Let's go."

"Don't you want to wash up or change your shirt?" I asked.

"It's not *my* shirt that's dirty," he said, pointing down at my T-shirt, which had come untucked again, revealing the stain. "Let's go." Timmy slammed the door shut behind him.

"Don't you have to lock it?" I asked.

"Why? There's nothing in there worth stealing. So again, what are you doing up so early?"

"Again, it's not early, and second, I was already out."

"Out where? Wait . . . did you go see that girl . . . what's her name?"

"Her name is Candice, and yeah, I did."

"Stupid. You gotta play it cool. You should have waited a day or two before you went chasing her," Timmy said.

"Like I need to take advice about girls from you," I chided him.

"What's wrong with taking it from me?" he asked. "I get more than my share of the babes . . . actually, I get some of *your* share as well. You're just lucky

I didn't decide I wanted that little Candice girl for myself."

"You? She's got way too much class for you!"

"Yeah, right. So how did it go?" Timmy asked.

"Not good."

"She blew you off?"

"Her father wouldn't let me see her," I mumbled.

"What?"

"He wouldn't let me see her. He told me to go away."

"What did you say to tick him off?"

"I didn't even get a chance to say anything. He answered the door and told me to go away."

"Why would he do that?" Timmy asked.

"He said I was a loser and he didn't want his daughter hanging around with a loser."

Timmy started laughing. Just the sort of support and understanding I was looking for.

Timmy pulled open the door of the Donut Hole. "After you . . . you loser," he said, bowing at the waist.

"Shut up or you'll be buying your own donut."

I walked into the smoke-filled donut shop. Most of the booths were filled—mostly with people who looked as though they hadn't slept last night. Red eyes, rumpled clothes, cigarette in one hand, coffee in the other. Some of them probably came straight here when the casino closed and were just killing time until it opened again.

"Next!" barked out the woman behind the counter.

I stepped forward. "Two coffees and a couple of donuts . . . What do you want, Timmy?"

"Double-chocolate," he said.

"Two double-chocolate donuts and a couple of coffees."

"*Large* coffees," Timmy added.

"Two large coffees," I echoed. "One just cream and the other double-double."

"Make that *triple-triple*," Timmy said. "That way I can get enough cream and sugar to keep me going until lunch."

The woman grunted out a response and went to fill the order.

I turned to Timmy. "I don't even know why we come here," I whispered. "The donuts and coffee all taste like cigarettes."

"That's one of the reasons I *like* coming here," Timmy said. "Besides, it's close and it's open."

"We should go to a real donut place."

"This is *real*," Timmy said. "Maybe the problem is it's too real for you."

"Too real? How can it be——?"

"Four-fifty," the woman said as she plopped down the donuts and the coffees. One of the coffees sloshed over the top and onto the counter. She didn't seem to notice, or maybe she just didn't care.

I handed her a five-dollar bill. "Keep the change," I said.

She grabbed it, grunted out something that might have been "Thank you" but could have just as easily been "Screw off," and walked away.

"It's the friendly service that keeps *me* coming back," Timmy said.

I pushed a lid down onto one of the coffees and Timmy did the same with the other. I grabbed one of the donuts. "Let's get out of here. I want to get away from the smoke."

"You know, that wouldn't be a problem if you took my advice and started smoking," Timmy said as he trailed after me out the door. "Instead of complaining, you could just inhale real deep, and it would be like getting your first smoke of the day for free."

"*You* inhale. I'm planning on using my lungs for a long time and I want 'em to keep working. Let's just go to the park and sit on a bench," I suggested.

Timmy peeled back the lid of his coffee and took a big sip. "Wrong one," he said, making a face. "No sugar," he explained, and we changed cups.

We walked across the grass of the park. It was soggy underfoot. That was partly the dew, and partly just from the mist that came off the Falls. We weren't even that close but the mist found its way to places far from the river.

The park was practically empty. Except for us, the only person around was some guy lying on a bench on the far side. Maybe he was sleeping it off, or maybe he just didn't have any money or a place to crash. We stopped at a picnic table and I sat down on one side, Timmy on the other. I sank my teeth into the donut. I was hungry, and the taste of the chocolate was still slightly stronger than that of the cigarette smoke.

Timmy had set down his coffee and pushed the last little bit of the donut into his mouth. He then pulled out a small pocketknife, opened it up, and started carving something in the table.

"Can I ask you a question?"

Timmy shrugged. "Ask away."

"Do you think . . . do you think I'm a loser?"

"You?" Timmy asked, sounding surprised.

That made me feel better. "Yeah, do you?"

"No way." He kept carving away at the table. "I *used* to think you were, though."

"Used to? What does that mean?"

"A long time ago. Like back in Grade 7."

"I'd just moved back here in Grade 7 . . . I didn't even *know* you," I said.

"I didn't know you either . . . not really."

"But if you didn't know me, how could you think I was a loser?"

"Well . . . I don't know," Timmy said. He kept cutting into the top of the table. It looked like he was carving his initials.

"Well, if you don't *know*, and you didn't even really *know* me, I don't know how you could think *anything* about me."

"It's just some of the things you said."

"I don't remember saying anything to you. We didn't start hanging out until Grade 8."

"It wasn't something you said to me, it was . . . it's nothing," he mumbled.

"It's got to be something. Just spit it out."

He didn't answer. He just kept digging the knife into the wood. He almost had the "T" completed.

"What did I say?" I asked.

Timmy looked up at me. "Do you remember Career Day?"

"Career Day? What are you talking about?"

"In Grade 7 they had a Career Day. People came in to talk to everybody about what they did for a living, and all the kids went and heard different people speak."

"Yeah . . . I guess I remember that . . . so what?"

"You and me were in one of the sessions together," Timmy said.

"Yeah, if you say so."

"And we each had to say what we wanted to be when we grew up. Do you remember?"

"I remember that—sort of—but I don't remember you being there. There were lots of kids in the group."

"I think there were like twenty or thirty," Timmy said. "Kids from all different classes."

"Well, obviously you remember me. What did I say?"

"You mostly just sat and listened while everybody talked about how they wanted to be a professional hockey player or a hairdresser or a rock star. When it was your turn you said you wanted to be an engineer," Timmy explained. "And I remember thinking, 'What sort of a goof would want to drive a train?'"

"Not a train driver, you idiot!" I snapped.

"I know that now. I found out later that it had to do with building things."

"That's a structural engineer," I said. "There's lots of different types. Chemical, medical, aerospace, mechanical—"

"Yeah, whatever,"Timmy interrupted. "That's when I started thinking you were a loser. At least driving a train made *some* sense."

"And what doesn't make sense about being an engineer?" I asked.

"How long you got to go to school to be one of those?" Timmy asked.

"I don't know. Five, maybe six or seven years of university, I guess."

"And how much does it cost to go to university for a year?"

"I don't know exactly. A lot of money."

"And to even get into one of those schools don't you have to have, like, really, really high marks?"

"I guess."

"So to become an engineer you have to be smart and have lots of money, right?"

"Yeah, probably," I answered.

"So, unless your mother's making a lot more money working at the casino than I think, you haven't got any money," Timmy said. "And unless I saw your last report card wrong, you ain't that smart, either."

"I do a lot better than you do!" I snapped.

"Big deal. *Everybody* does a lot better than I do. Being smarter than me isn't something that's gonna win you a medal . . . or get you into engineer school."

Maybe my marks weren't that high, but I did pass every subject, and I was good at math, and if I really did work harder I knew I could bring my marks up and . . . who was I kidding?

"What do you want to be now?" Timmy asked.

I shrugged and shook my head. "I don't know."

"Me neither, and that's why neither of us is a loser."

"What are you talking about?" I asked.

"Before, you had all these dreams about being some sort of engineer, right?"

"Yeah."

"And now you don't, right?"

"Not anymore."

"And that's why you aren't a loser anymore."

"Let me get this straight," I said. "When I had dreams, I was a loser. Now I don't have dreams, I'm not a loser."

"Exactly!" Timmy stuck his knife into the table to punctuate his point. "The only losers I know are the guys who aren't smart enough to know that there's no point in having a dream that isn't going to come true. The ones who believe they have a chance to make something of themselves, they're the real losers."

"You're kidding me, right?"

Timmy shook his head. "Look around. Who do you know who made it?"

"Made it?"

"Got their dream."

"Some people get the things they dream about," I argued.

"Yeah? Name one."

"Well . . . people on TV, or that you read about in the newspaper or—"

"I'm talking about *real* people, people from here, people you know. Name one, just one."

"How about the Jamisons?" I asked.

"They won a frigging lottery!" Timmy exclaimed. "And not even the big prize, just fifty thousand dollars! And besides, all they really did with the money was buy a second-hand car that kept breaking down and a double-wide trailer. Is that your idea of making it . . . to end up in a double-wide trailer?"

"No, it's just—"

"You're not a loser," Tim said. "Just don't start get-ting any stupid ideas."

"Wanting more than this is stupid?"

"Wanting it isn't. That's human nature. Thinking you have a chance to get it . . . now that's stupid."

"You know what *is* stupid?"

"What?" Timmy asked.

"You!"

"Hey, don't get mad at me for telling you the truth," he said.

"You wouldn't know the truth if it bit you in the butt!" I snapped.

"Look around," Timmy said. "Nobody from here ever gets anywhere else. Nobody makes it."

"I'm not from around here," I said.

"You're not? You were born here."

"But I left."

"And you came *back*. That's even worse. Get real."

"I am real. More real than you, saying that nobody from here ever makes it."

"I'm not talking about somebody who got a job at the casino, or working in the Ripley's Museum, or some guy who's the night manager at some stupid hotel barely making minimum wage. I'm talking about somebody who *really* made it."

I got up from the bench. "Well maybe I'm going to be the first."

"You?" he asked, and he chuckled.

"Why not me?"

"A better question is 'Why you?' What makes you think that you're better than everybody else? What makes you think you can make it when nobody else can? You think you're better than everybody else?"

"Maybe."

"Then maybe you *are* a loser," Timmy said.

"Screw you!"

"No thanks, you're not my type."

"Screw off!" I yelled, and then I turned and started walking away.

"Real clever!" Timmy screamed. "That's the type of language I think of when I think of an engineer!"

I kept walking, not looking back, but I held up one hand with the middle finger raised.

"Hey!" Timmy yelled. "I got just one question!"

I stopped and turned around. "Yeah? What is it?"

"Bobby's older brother got him a two-four of brew. Me and him talked about splitting it. We're gonna meet up behind the power plant around seven. You coming?"

I wanted to tell him to screw off again. I wanted to go back and knock that knife out of his hand and smack him across the face. I wanted to do a lot of things.

"I'll see you at seven," I said, and then I turned and walked away.

"And don't be too late or there'll just be empty bottles for you to sniff!"

I didn't answer. I just kept walking.

"Hey, Jay!" Timmy screamed, and I looked back over my shoulder. "Thanks for the breakfast, man!"

CHAPTER THREE

WHEN I OPENED THE DOOR I could hear music and smell oatmeal cooking. Both were sure signs that my mother was awake and up.

"Hello!" I yelled out.

"Good morning, Jay!" she answered. "Come and join me for breakfast!"

"I've already eaten!" I said and continued up the stairs.

"Hang on!" she yelled.

I stopped on the top step and she appeared at the bottom of the stairs. She was wearing a ratty old housecoat and her hair was in curlers.

"I want to talk. Come and sit with me while I eat."

I never liked those *I want to talk* conversations. That never signalled anything good. I paused for a second, and then thumped back down the stairs.

"Take it easy!" my mother said. "I want you to come *down* the stairs, not *through* the stairs!"

"Sorry."

"There's enough to fix up around here without you breaking the stairs."

"If I broke 'em, I'd fix 'em," I said as I continued down at a more gentle pace.

She met me at the bottom with a hug. I figured I was getting too big to be hugged all the time, but it still felt good. Besides, a hug meant that whatever she wanted to talk about wasn't something I'd done wrong.

"I know you'd fix them. I don't know what we'd do if you weren't here to do all the work that needs to be done."

She let me go and I followed her down the hall to the kitchen. There was oatmeal bubbling away on the stove and a lit cigarette perched in an ashtray on the table.

"I thought you were quitting," I said as I walked over and turned down the radio. Country music gave me a headache *and* indigestion.

"I did quit." She gave a sad little smile. "I quit between each cigarette."

"That wasn't even funny the first time I heard it."

"It's not easy." She stubbed out the cigarette in the ashtray. "That was my last one, promise."

"You shouldn't make promises you can't keep," I warned her.

"This time is different. I'm trying something new."

"I thought you'd already tried everything . . . gum, nicotine patches, acupuncture."

"Hypnosis . . . I'm going to be hypnotized."

"You're joking, right?"

"No. There's a hypnotist performing in the lounge this week. He's really very nice, and—"

"You think everybody is nice," I said.

"Not everybody."

"Almost everybody."

She walked over to the stove and gave the oatmeal a stir. "Regardless, he said he's had great success in helping people stop smoking."

"He's a nightclub hypnotist. He's probably had more success making people cluck like chickens."

"Then we have nothing to lose," my mother said.

"What do you mean?"

"Either I stop smoking, or he convinces me I'm a chicken and we have a steady supply of eggs for breakfast. Speaking of which, what exactly did you have for breakfast?"

"Coffee and a donut."

"That's not enough for a growing boy. You need more than that."

"There was cream in my coffee. Does that count as a dairy product?"

She burst out laughing. I could always make her laugh. "I don't know what I'd do without you," she said. She put a bowl of oatmeal down in front of me.

"But I've already had—"

"Not another word!" she exclaimed. "Eat!"

I tried to get up out of my chair and she stopped me.

"I was just going to get a spoon," I said. "Unless you want me to eat it with my fingers."

"I'll get you a spoon." She opened up a drawer and pulled out two, one for each of us.

"You said you wanted to talk," I said. Whatever it was, I just wanted to get it started so it could end. I hated waiting.

"Yes," my mother said. "You must have come in pretty late last night."

"Earlier than you."

"I didn't have any choice. My shift ran until almost three in the morning. So what time did you get in?" she asked.

"I'm not sure. I don't have a watch and I didn't look at the clock."

"It had to be after one-thirty because I called and there was no answer," she said.

"It might have been a lot earlier. I could have been asleep already. You know I can't hear the phone from my room."

She took a long sip from her coffee. I didn't think she believed me, but there was nothing she could do about it.

"Do you know what tonight is?" my mother asked.

"Friday night."

"It's more than just Friday night."

"The first Friday night of the summer?" I asked.

"That too, but more important. I thought you'd know," she said, sounding disappointed.

"I do know."

"You do?"

I nodded. "It's your anniversary. Five years sober."

"You remembered!" she exclaimed.

"Of course. I was going to get you a card, but Hallmark doesn't seem to make one that covers this occasion."

"They should. Do you have an idea how many alcoholics and recovering alcoholics there are in this country?"

"I know exactly how many there are because you keep telling me," I explained.

"At the meeting tonight I get my five-year medallion."

"You're not working?" I asked. This was possibly going to put a wrench in my plans to be out late again.

"I'm going to work my shift after the meeting. I've got nine to three in the morning again."

So much for having to come in early. I could stay out as late as I wanted.

"And because it's a special night, the meeting is open."

"Closed" meant that nobody but AA people could attend. "Open" meant that anybody could come to the meeting . . . oh, no.

"Family and friends are allowed to come," my mother said. "And since you're all the family I have, I was really hoping that you could—"

"But I have plans," I said, cutting her off.

"Plans?"

"Yeah, Timmy and I were going to . . . going to . . . you know . . . hang out together. Do I really have to come?" I begged.

My mother sighed and got that sad, drowned kitten look. "You don't *have* to come," she said. "I don't want to force you. It's just that it's a big night for me, and you're not just my family, you're the reason I stopped drinking, and—"

"What time is the meeting?"

"It starts at seven. It should be over by eight or eight-thirty at the latest."

"But half the night is gone by then," I protested.

"I guess that depends on how late you're planning to get home," she said.

"Where is this meeting?" I asked. I'd learned that there were Alcoholics Anonymous meetings every night of the week, and more than just one meeting each night.

"Tonight's is in the basement of St. James United Church."

That wasn't too bad. That was at least on the way to where Timmy and I were going to meet.

"It's just that those meetings really creep me out," I explained.

"I don't understand. Everybody is always so nice."

"*Too* nice," I said. "Everybody keeps coming up and wanting to talk and shake hands, and everybody acts like they're everybody else's best friend."

"There are worse things than being friendly. Besides, we *are* like a family, and since you're my son they consider you part of the family too."

"Don't you think that's creepy?" I asked.

"I think it's creepy to think what would have been our future without AA and those people."

"Okay, I know it helped, but I don't understand why you have to keep going."

"I have to keep going because I'm an alcoholic."

"You haven't had a drink for five years. Doesn't that mean you *were* an alcoholic?" I asked.

"I *am* an alcoholic," she said. "A *recovering* alcoholic, and without the support of my sponsor and the other members I might lose the recovering part. They keep me going, one day at—"

"Yeah, at a time, I know," I said. I'd heard that line a couple of million times . . . of course, one at a time.

"Well?" my mother asked. "Are you going to come to the meeting?"

"I don't want to be there . . . but I will . . . for you."

She got up and came over and gave me a hug. I thought I deserved more than a hug for doing this. Maybe a twenty-dollar bill and a new T-shirt . . . or at least a clean one.

CHAPTER FOUR

"IS IT GOING TO START SOON?" I whispered to my mother as I looked around the room. The entire basement of the church was filled with rows and rows of wooden chairs, and almost every chair was taken.

"It's still a minute or two before seven. We don't like to close the doors until we have to. We wouldn't want anybody to see the closed doors and leave."

"They could always open it themselves, or knock."

"You have no idea how difficult it is to come through that door the first time. That's why it needs to be open, so they'll know they're welcome."

I was going to offer some smart-ass comment, but really, I knew better. I was surrounded by AA people, and some of them took this stuff way too seriously. It was like it was a religion or something.

I looked back at the doors. There were still people coming in, and each person was greeted with a handshake or a hug. Strange. These people had probably seen each other at the meeting the night before, and the one the night before that, and the night before that . . . so why the big hellos? Some people went to a meeting every night, seven nights a week, week after week, month after month, year after year. Instead of being addicted to alcohol, they were addicted to AA meetings. I guess there were worse things. And the meetings weren't just for the locals. People who were on vacation, or who'd just come to town for the day, could attend too. Man, looking at the Falls was boring, but it beat the heck out of coming to one of these meetings.

I scanned the room. Most of the people here were familiar. Some I'd seen around town, and some I actually knew. I recognized lots and lots of people who worked with my mother at the casino. There were so many of them, I wondered if the casino would only hire you if you checked a box that said "Alcoholic" on the job application. There were also teachers from my school, a fireman who worked at the station at the bottom of our street, a lawyer who had his office above the bank, a teller from the bank, the guy who was my soccer coach the last year I played, and a couple of cops. Was it really a good idea for people who had a drinking problem to be carrying guns? Well, at least, hopefully, they weren't drinking now.

My eye met that of our neighbour from down the street, and he gave me a little wave. Reluctantly I waved and looked away. If this was supposed to be

Alcoholics *Anonymous*, wouldn't it make more sense if everybody wore a mask over their face? There was nothing anonymous about being here. If it was me, I wouldn't want everybody to know who I was. It wasn't like this was something to be proud of. It was just so strange seeing all these people here. The only thing I could think of that might be weirder was all of us meeting at a nudist colony. At least here I had someplace to put my hands.

"Hello, Leanne. Hello, Jay." It was Mrs. Bayliss, my mother's sponsor. She was the person my mother would call—day or night—if she had the urge to drink. She was also a teacher at my school. She was always friendly and said hello to me around the school, which made things even more uncomfortable.

"I didn't think you were going to make it. I was starting to get a bit worried," my mother told her.

"Things got a little hectic." She squeezed by me and took the seat my mother had been saving for her. "You nervous?" she asked my mother.

"Not anymore. Thanks for coming."

"I wouldn't miss this for the world," she said, and turned to me. "And it's so good to see you, Jay. You must be very proud of your mother."

"Yeah . . . proud."

"Five years is a major accomplishment," Mrs. Bayliss said.

"I feel very proud," my mother said. "How many years has it been for you now?"

"In September it will be twenty-three years."

"Twenty-three years!" I exclaimed. "And you keep coming to these meetings?"

"It doesn't matter if it's twenty-three minutes, twenty-three days, or twenty-three years," she said. "An alcoholic is always an alcoholic."

"That's what I hear," I said.

She furrowed her brow. "It sounds like you don't completely believe it."

I shrugged. "You'd know better than me."

A loud voice called out, "Good evening!" and all eyes turned to the front. There was a man in a suit standing at a podium.

"Hello. It's so good to see so many familiar faces, and so many new faces, perhaps coming out for the first time, or the first time in a long time. I will be chairing tonight's meeting. My name is Frank, and I'm an alcoholic."

"Hello, Frank!" called out a hundred voices.

Just once I'd have liked somebody to start off by saying something like, "Hi, I'm Barney, and I'm an alien," or ". . . I suffer from indigestion," or ". . . I have bad breath," or ". . . my mother dropped me on my head when I was a baby," and everybody would answer back something like, "Drop dead, Barney." Just once I'd have liked that to happen.

"Could we all stand for a moment of silent prayer," Frank said. There was a chorus of chairs scraping against the floor as everybody rose. I stumbled to my feet.

Cautiously I raised my head and looked down the row. Everybody had their heads down, eyes closed, in silent prayer. I knew what I was praying for—that this meeting wouldn't last forever.

"Thank you," Frank said. "Next, I'd like to lead you in the Serenity Prayer. 'God grant me the serenity to accept the things I cannot change,'" he began, and everybody in the room joined in with him, "'the courage to change the things I can, and wisdom to know the difference. Amen.'"

Frank raised a glass from the podium and took a big drink. It was probably water, but it could just as well have been gin or vodka . . . that would have been funny.

"There was a time," Frank started to say, "when the most important things in my life all came out of a whisky bottle."

"You tell it straight, Frank!" yelled a voice.

"Back then I couldn't tell it straight. If you'd asked me, I would have told you that my wife and my kids were what mattered to me, but I'd have been lying. And I proved that lie every day when I put them all through pain and suffering to satisfy my need for alcohol. Thank the Lord that when I hit rock bottom on that fateful day they were still there, that I hadn't driven them completely away, that they still loved me and forgave me. Their love, and the power of God, pulled me out of that whisky bottle and let me lead the life I'm now living."

"We're proud of ya, Frankie!" called another voice, and people began to cheer and clap.

"Could we now have our reading from the Big Book," Frank said.

A woman walked up the aisle toward the front. In her hands was the "Big Book," sort of the bible for AA. She and Frank hugged and then she took his place at the podium, setting the book down in front of her.

"My name is Sharon, and I'm an alcoholic."

"Hello, Sharon!" called out the audience.

I should have yelled back, "I'm Jay, and I'm not, and I'm tired of hearing about it!" But of course I didn't.

"For years I wasn't comfortable in my own skin," Sharon began. "I tried to run and hide, but I couldn't run and hide from myself. Wherever I went, there I was. Same person, same problems, same addiction. It doesn't matter if you're an alcoholic living in Toronto, or New York, or Niagara Falls, you're still an alcoholic. One day, praise the Lord, I hit rock bottom, and there were people there to help me make the climb back up . . . the climb I continue to make, one day at a time."

"There's no other way!" called out a voice.

"Let me read from the Big Book," she said, as she opened up the book and flipped through the pages. "'Rarely have we seen a person fail who has thoroughly followed our path,'" she began to read.

I looked over at my mother. She had her copy of the book open on her lap, as did others sitting around us. As Sharon continued to read, my mother followed along in the book, her finger tracing the words, line by line.

"'Our stories disclose in a general way what we used to be like, what happened, and what we are like now,'" she continued to read. "'If you have decided you want what we have and are willing to go to any length to get it—then you are ready to take certain steps.'"

The steps . . . the Twelve Steps. I knew all about the Twelve Steps. The Twelve Steps were like the Ten Commandments of AA, except that instead of "thou shalt not"s there were a bunch of things you had to do.

"'Here are the steps we took, which are suggested as a program for recovery,'" Sharon continued. "'One. We admitted we were powerless over alcohol—that our lives had become unmanageable. Two. Came to believe that a Power greater than ourselves could restore us to sanity. Three. Made a decision to turn our will and our lives over to the care of God as we understood him.'"

Actually, almost all the steps had to do with God. AA was sort of a combination self-help group, church, and religion all rolled into one—not that I knew much about churches or religion. I really hadn't seen the inside of many churches except for the ones I saw on Sunday mornings when I was clicking around the dial looking for cartoons.

"'And finally, twelve. Having had a spiritual awakening as the result of these steps, we tried to carry this message to alcoholics, and to practise these principles in all our affairs.'"

As she continued to read, I heard somebody sobbing from behind me and off to the side. I wanted to look, but I didn't want to be too obvious about it. Slowly, I turned my head. It was a man—he looked like a biker, all dressed in leathers with a big old beard and beer belly—standing in the corner, crying. Two people—a man in a suit, and a little old woman who was old enough to be his grandmother, and small enough to be his lunch—had both wrapped their arms around him, offering comfort. Where in the world would you ever see those three together except at a place like this?

There was a round of applause and Sharon made her way back down the aisle. As she walked, people stood up and shook her hand. She finally reached her seat.

"No matter how many times I hear the Twelve Steps, I still find them moving," Frank said from the podium.

Personally, the more I heard them the more I wanted to move farther away so I wouldn't have to hear them anymore.

"I'll now read the Twelve Traditions of AA," Frank said. "No meeting is complete until we have read the Twelve and Twelve."

I almost wanted to laugh—"the Twelve and Twelve" sounded like a case of beer . . . twelve Coors and twelve Coors Light. I wondered what brand of beer Bobby's brother had got for us. Wouldn't it be strange if it was that two-four?

"Before getting to the announcements, I'd like to remind people that while we live with yesterday, today, and tomorrow, it is only today that matters. Yesterday is gone, and while we remember, we must let it go. Tomorrow is just a dream. We live for today, and take each day as it comes . . . one day at a time," Frank said. "Does anybody have any announcements they'd like to share?"

A man sitting just in front of me put up his hand.

"I recognize our good friend Jerry."

A man stood up. "Thanks, Frank. I wanted to remind people that there are still spots available on our bus trip to the annual general meeting in Cleveland in July."

"Are there many spaces?" Frank asked.

"So far, twenty-seven members have committed. We have three more places on the bus."

"I'd like to add," a woman standing at the back said, "that having been to three conventions I can guarantee it will be inspirational . . . and fun. I just wish I could go to this one myself."

"Thank you for that endorsement," Frank said. "So, anybody interested should see Jerry as soon as possible. If there are no other announcements I'm delighted to move on to the most joyful part of our evening. Would Phil and Susan please come forward."

A couple—they looked to be in their forties or fifties—stood up and walked to the front, hand in hand, as the audience cheered.

"This is pretty special," Frank began. "Phil and Susan, who have been married for a little less than four years, are celebrating nine months of sobriety. Here are your nine-month chips."

The crowd roared out its approval while Frank handed first one, and then the other, a little red thing that looked like a poker chip.

"Hello, I'm Phil."

"And I'm Susan," his wife added.

"And we're alcoholics," they both said together.

"Hello, Phil. Hello, Susan."

Phil and Susan started to tell their story, about how alcohol had been their enemy and being dry had saved their lives and their marriage. People cheered, and then Phil and Susan returned to their seats. They were replaced by some people who had been sober for six months, then two months, and finally those people who had been sober for the grand total of one month.

With each speaker it was just more of the same. Different people with different names, saying the same things with slightly different words. Same song, different melody. The amazing thing was that people cheered each speaker as if they were hearing these stories for the first time. Maybe all that alcohol these people had consumed before they'd stopped drinking had impaired their short-term memory.

"I see many new faces in the audience," Frank said. "Is there anybody who wishes to declare a desire to stop drinking?"

There was silence as people looked around, but nobody moved. Then the big biker dude was making his way up from the back of the room. He walked up the aisle hand in hand with the little old woman. At the podium she reached up and gave him a hug before retreating down the aisle, leaving him alone in front of the crowd.

There wasn't a sound as everybody waited for him to begin. He looked down at his feet. He looked like he was shaking. Finally Frank walked over and put his mouth right by the guy's ear. I wondered what he was saying. The big biker nodded along in agreement with whatever it was. Frank moved away.

The biker cleared his throat and then began. "My name is . . . my name is Cole . . . and . . . and I'm an alcoholic."

"Hello, Cole!" the audience sang out.

"I never thought I'd be in one of these meetings," Cole said quietly. His voice was as small as he was large, and I had to strain to hear him. "I thought AA meetings were for losers."

Loser—that word hit me in the side of the head.

"And maybe I *am* a loser," he continued. "I lost everything." He started shaking more and there was a catch in his voice. "Last night I got drunk . . . again. This time was different, though. I got drunk so I wouldn't feel the bullet. I wasn't gonna wake up with no hangover . . . I was gonna wake up dead. I didn't think anybody would care."

"I care!" called out a man.

"We all care!" a woman agreed.

"And when I did wake up, I realized . . . I realized . . . that I *was* killing myself. Maybe not with a gun . . . but with the bottle . . . and I decided I needed help . . . that I wasn't strong enough to get better on my own."

"None of us are!" called up a voice.

"You're not alone!" said another voice.

The man started crying—not just a few little tears crying, but big, projectile tears, sobbing, shaking, crying.

I felt a wave of anxiousness. It was like I was seeing something that I shouldn't be seeing, witnessing something too private and personal. I felt like I was looking into the window of somebody's house . . . no, worse . . . I was looking inside *him*.

Suddenly people materialized all around the biker and he was escorted away from the podium and enveloped in a group hug.

Frank returned to the podium. "Our new friend, Cole, has expressed his wish to stop drinking, and he will be given a desire chip and the support to help make that desire a reality. Cole has already admitted that he is powerless over alcohol . . . he is part of the way along the Twelve Steps. Thank you for giving testimony." Frank paused and took a big drink, draining his glass. "And now something I've been looking forward to all night. A special time. Not only for the person it involves, but for the inspiration it offers to the rest of us gathered here. Could Leanne and her sponsor, Sarah, please come forward."

My mother and Mrs. Bayliss stood up. As my mother passed by she reached down and gave my hand a little squeeze. They made their way to the front accompanied by a chorus of cheers and shouts and hugs and handshakes. I sank even further into my seat. This was all embarrassing.

"Hello, my name is Sarah, and I'm an alcoholic," Mrs. Bayliss began. "I know most of the people here, and you know my story, so I'll try to keep it short."

I didn't know her story, but I couldn't imagine it was much different from anybody else's story. I was just grateful for the keeping it short part.

"Growing up, I always tried to make people happy, to do the right thing, to do my best. But no matter how well I did, I never felt it was good enough. Even when I won I didn't win by enough. Even when I did better than other people it wasn't enough. I was empty inside, and no amount of success could fill that emptiness. I thought if I moved, my life would be better someplace else, but it wasn't. So I moved again, and it was no better. Wherever I was, it was part of me. That emptiness. And I turned to alcohol to try and fill that hole that wouldn't let me be complete.

"At first I drank just a little. It filled the void, and eased my nerves, and quieted that little voice in my head that said I wasn't good enough. And then the little became a little more."

I looked at my watch. So much for keeping it short. So much for me getting out of here on time. And all this talk about drinking was making me antsy . . . nothing a drink or two wouldn't solve, but what if all the beer was gone when I got there?

"And I kept drinking. One drink was too much and ten drinks weren't enough. But I told myself I didn't have a drinking problem."

"Nobody thinks they do," somebody said, and other people yelled out in agreement.

"How could I have a drinking problem?" she asked. "I had never been arrested, or fired from a job. I was a teacher, and I went to school every day. Of course, that didn't stop me from being drunk the entire summer." She paused. "It was amazing how fast summer holidays could go when you were drunk as a skunk for eight weeks."

There was a roar of laughter from the audience.

"Then I came home from school one day to find my husband had left me. His note said he couldn't handle the drinking. What did he know? And then I was at school and fell down flat on my face in the cafeteria. I told them I had the flu and wasn't feeling well. I just hoped nobody could smell the 'flu' that I'd caught out of a gin bottle. And when the principal offered to have somebody drive me home, I said I'd be fine. That's when the accident happened."

Suddenly the quiet in the room got even quieter. There wasn't a sound. Not coughing, or people shuffling in their seats, or even a chair moving. It was like every person in the room was holding their breath. I sat up in my seat and leaned forward. Maybe she'd told this story before, but *I'd* never heard it.

"I almost killed two people that day. A young girl and myself. She lived, and I was reborn, because that was the last time I drank."

There was a round of applause.

"Now I'd like to talk about something very special. This day marks the five-year anniversary of sobriety for one of our members . . . one of our friends . . . one of our family. I'd like you all to give a round of applause for Leanne."

People started cheering and hooting and whistling. I clapped my hands.

"Hello, my name is Leanne, and I'm an alcoholic," my mother said, and the whole audience—including me this time—said hello back.

"Five years. It's hard to believe. If you'd asked me back then if I'd be here tonight I would have said no. That first day, I didn't know if I could make it to a second. But I kept going, one day at a time." She reached into her pocket and pulled something out. "I'm not so good at math so I figured it out, right here," she said, holding up a small piece of paper for everybody to see. "There have been one thousand, eight hundred, and twenty-six one-day-at-a-times . . . that's how many days there are in five years when one of those years is a leap year."

People chuckled.

"And there are some reasons why I've been sober all that time and why I hope I'll wake up sober tomorrow morning. There's been my sponsor . . . my good friend, Sarah."

My mother started clapping and the audience joined in. Mrs. Bayliss looked down at the ground, embarrassed but happy. I once heard that embarrassment is just happiness trying to leak out.

"And all of my friends—my family—here at AA who have helped me understand so much and who support me each and every day. And finally, there is my son. Could you please stand up, Jay?"

I felt a hot rush throughout my entire body.

"Don't be shy," she said. "Could you please come up here?"

Slowly I rose to my feet, aware that every eye in the whole room was now on me. If I'd known she was going to do that there's no way in the world I would have agreed to come tonight. Carefully I side-shuffled along the row of seats to reach the aisle. Head down, I walked to the front until I was standing at my mother's side.

"Jay," she said, "thanks for standing by me and for giving me the reason to join AA to begin with."

She wrapped her arms around me and started crying. I felt so stupid, standing in front of this roomful of people, her crying and holding on to me. Worst of all, I thought I might start crying as well.

"And what would an anniversary be without a celebration?" Frank announced. *"Happy birth-daaay toooo you,"* he started to sing, and everybody joined in as two women, holding a big cake with five candles on top, walked up the aisle. My mother stopped hugging me but still held on to one hand. If she hadn't been holding that hand I would have scrambled away.

The women stopped right in front of my mother just as the song ended. My mother took a big breath and blew out the candles, and there was another round of applause. Didn't these people ever get tired of cheering?

"I'd like to invite everybody to stay after our meeting for coffee and a piece of cake," Frank announced. He turned to my mother. "Could you lead us in our closing prayer?"

Everybody stood and bowed their heads.

"Our Father who art in Heaven," my mother started, and everybody joined in.

It was about the only prayer I knew. I bowed my head as well. "Hallowed be thy name. Thy Kingdom come. Thy will be done, on earth as it is in Heaven . . ."

CHAPTER FIVE

"YOU MUST BE SO PROUD of your mother," the woman said as she reached the front of the line. I nodded and handed her a piece of cake. She picked up a plastic spoon off the table.

I was part of an assembly line. My mother cut her "birthday cake"—that's what they called it at AA because she was "reborn" the day she stopped drinking. Then she handed it to Mrs. Bayliss to put on a paper plate, who passed it on to me to hand out to the people waiting in line. Luckily it was a big cake because there were a lot of people, and a couple had already come back for seconds.

Standing there, giving everybody cake, I had no choice but to talk to people. Just a few words, but everybody wanted to talk. These AA people were just about the friendliest people in the world. And as I listened and nodded my head and mumbled back a few words, I watched.

It was the strangest collection of people you'd ever want to see. With most sorts of groups the people would all look kind of the same. Maybe they'd be the same age, or all male or female, or all white or black, or maybe they'd all dress in golf clothes. There was usually something that you could see that they had in common. It wasn't like that with these AA people. Male and female, every age from about twenty to senior citizens, suits and track pants and shorts and skirts and leather pants, white, black, brown, and Asian, businessmen and bikers and bums who looked like they'd slept on the street. I figured alcoholism didn't discriminate.

A couple of times I was positive I could smell alcohol on somebody's breath as they leaned close to talk. I guess for some "one day at a time" started tomorrow, or skipped a day here and there.

Almost without exception each person took their piece of cake and proceeded through the big, open double doors leading to the courtyard. I could see people out there, sitting, eating, and talking. And, of course, smoking. Not everybody smoked but it was amazing just how many of them did. It was like they were thinking that since their liver wasn't going to kill them now they might as well go to the next available organ and burn out their lungs. For some of them I figured it was time to stop coming to so many AA meetings and start trying to find a Smokenders group instead.

The smoke wafted in through the open doors and permeated the church's basement. I hated the smell of smoke. If there was a Hell the flames would smell like cigarettes.

I glanced at my watch again. It was almost eight-thirty. My mother had to be leaving soon if she was going to get to work on time. Being on time for me wasn't going to happen. By the time I got out of here and up to the power station I was going to be really late, and most of the beer would be gone already. Actually, knowing Timmy and Bobby the way I did, it might *all* be gone. Wouldn't that be a kick in the teeth—this AA meeting would be keeping *one* person from drinking tonight . . . me! My drinking problem would be that I had nothing to drink. Just the thought of that was making me want to bolt for the door.

"That's everybody," Mrs. Bayliss said. "And that means that this piece is for you." She handed me a plate. There were also pieces for both her and my mother. The three of us were the only people left inside the hall.

"Are you missing school?" Mrs. Bayliss asked me.

"Are you joking?" I exclaimed.

She laughed. "Mostly. You may not believe this, but the only people who look forward to summer vacation more than the students are the teachers."

"Then you must *really* look forward to the summer," I said, and both she and my mother laughed.

"You know, I heard some good things about you, just the other day," she said.

"You did?"

"Don't sound so surprised."

"Who were you talking to?" my mother asked.

"Gus Green."

"My shop teacher?"

"And my neighbour."

"Jay got a great mark in auto shop," my mother said. "Wasn't it a ninety-one?"

"Ninety-three," I corrected her.

"Gus says you have a real talent."

"Jay has always been really good with cars—actually, anything with a motor. I don't think I could even keep my old heap on the road if it wasn't for his help."

"I don't know the first thing about cars," Mrs. Bayliss said. "If the engine makes a funny noise I just turn up the radio."

That sounded like most of the people in my class. My marks were so good because most of the other people were stupid when it came to engines. A lot of the jokers in my class couldn't even figure how to release the hood, let alone know what to do if they ever managed to open it.

It also didn't hurt that I liked Gus—he let me call him Gus. If I was late for class I could make it up by walking in with a couple of coffees. He liked his done the same as Timmy, with three creams and three sugars. And if there were problems in the class he didn't send people to the office, he dealt with it himself.

There was one class where a couple of guys—older guys who should have been in Grade 12—started challenging him. It looked like it might come to blows. Gus just reached behind the counter and pulled out a good-sized piece of pipe and told them to sit down, shut up, screw off, or get smashed. They decided it was time to sit down. Gus was cool. Way too cool to be a teacher.

"When Jay was ten he built a go-kart," my mother said. "And after that there were mini-bikes. He could have a great future as a mechanic."

"Gus thinks more than that . . . not that there's anything wrong with being a mechanic. Good money, honest work, and who doesn't need a good mechanic?" Mrs. Bayliss said. "Gus said that Jay understands the bigger picture—those were his words—not only how to fix things but how they work, and how they could be designed to work better."

"What did he think Jay could be?" my mother asked.

"He said he thought Jay could be a great engineer."

"That's what Jay wants to be!" my mother exclaimed.

"You do?" Mrs. Bayliss asked.

"I *did*."

"But now you don't?"

I shook my head.

"What made you change your mind?" she asked.

"Things change. I wanted to be a garbage man and a cowboy once, too."

"That cowboy thing sounds promising, but maybe you should think about engineering again. I know it would take a lot of work and time . . ."

"Five years of university," I said. I had a strange feeling of déjà vu. This was a warped version of the conversation I'd just had with Timmy.

"It sounds like a long time, but——"

"And a lot of money. A whole lot of money," I said, cutting her off.

"Yes, it would be," Mrs. Bayliss said, shaking her head slightly.

"I'll do whatever I have to do to help," my mother said.

"Unless you're going to start *winning* at blackjack instead of dealing, it's a lot more money than you can raise," I pointed out.

"There are also loans and even scholarships available to good students," Mrs. Bayliss said.

"Yeah, good students . . . like that applies to me."

"It could," Mrs. Bayliss said.

I wanted to ask who was fooling who, but I didn't want to waste any more time. There might still be two or three beers left if I hurried. The longer I was here the more I needed those beers.

"I was also hoping to ask you about something," Mrs. Bayliss asked. "Do you have a couple of minutes?"

"Um . . . not really . . . I'm already late."

"Speaking of late, I'd better get going myself," my mother said. "I don't want to get fired . . . especially if I'm going to be saving up for engineering school." She and Mrs. Bayliss hugged. "Thanks for everything," my mother said.

"Come on, I'll walk you out," I offered.

"I've got an idea," Mrs. Bayliss said. "How about if I drive you where you're going, and then I can ask my question and you won't be any later than you already are?"

That had to be the worst idea I'd ever heard in my entire—

"What a wonderful offer!" my mother said. She gave me a hug and then hurried down the aisle and was gone.

"So where am I driving you to?"

"That's okay," I said. "I don't want to put you out."

"I've got nothing else on my schedule. I was just going home to watch TV."

The last thing in the world I wanted was for anybody to see me being driven around by one of the teachers from my high school. That was even worse than my mother driving me. Besides, how could I explain to Mrs. Bayliss that I was headed for a bush party behind the power station?

"I'm not going far. Just to Timmy's," I lied. "Maybe you could ask me that question before I go."

"Don't want to be seen with one of your high school teachers, huh?"

"Well . . ."

"I understand. I'll be quick. I was wondering if you've ever thought of getting involved in Alateen."

"Alateen?"

"It's a group run by AA for teenagers who—"

"I don't have a drinking problem!" I exclaimed.

"I didn't say you did."

"I don't even drink!" I lied.

She shot me a look of disbelief, and I stared down at the floor.

"Alateen is for teenagers who have a parent who has a drinking problem."

"My mother doesn't have a drinking problem . . . not anymore."

She smiled. "Your mother is still an alcoholic and she always will be."

"That part doesn't make sense."

"It doesn't make sense to a lot of alcoholics, either. That's why they start drinking again, because they forget."

My mother wasn't going to start drinking again. I didn't have to worry about that—at least, not the way I used to worry about it.

"Alateen is a group of teenagers, led by a counsellor, who talk about their shared experiences coping with an alcoholic parent," she said.

"Coping?"

"Problems that it caused them, difficult times, things that they had to do for their parents, things that their parents should have done for them but didn't."

I shook my head. "I didn't have any of those."

"Denial is the hardest part."

"I'm not denying anything. I gotta go."

I started to walk away and she reached out and grabbed my arm. "I just want you to know that there's help out there if you ever want it. Okay?"

I nodded. She let go of my arm and I turned and walked away, quickly, not looking back, just hoping she wasn't going to call out to me.

CHAPTER SIX

I THREADED MY WAY through the throng of people crowding the sidewalk. There were parents with little kids in tow, groups of Japanese tourists all following dutifully behind their guide, flashing away with their cameras, single men and women, and groups of teenagers in town for the night, looking for excitement, or trouble . . . or both.

It was now just on the edge between day and night. The neon signs that had been lit up for hours were starting to glow brighter in contrast to the darkness settling in around us. The signs offered flashing glimpses of excitement—food, drink, entertainment, gambling. Even though I'd walked down this street a million times, it still sent a little rush up my spine. I knew that the signs were mainly just hype, but it was flashing, multicoloured, brilliantly bright hype.

I looked up in time to see the fake volcano rumbling on top of one of the buildings, threatening to shower the people with fake lava. There were a lot of things along the strip that were fake.

I stopped for a few seconds to watch my personal favourite. It was a mechanical mannequin dressed in circus tights moving along a tightrope stretched high above the traffic. Slowly, foot over foot, he made his way across the street. I couldn't help thinking that it would be quite the view from up there. I loved high places. Besides, I thought, with a little training, I could learn to walk a tightrope or—

"Sorry," a man said as he bumped into me.

Instinctively I put my hand down to my pocket to check for my wallet. That was a trick pickpockets used, bumping into you so they could lift your wallet. Mine was still there.

"I was so busy looking up," he said, gesturing to the tightrope walker above our heads, "that I wasn't watching where I was going."

"That's okay," I mumbled in response. "I was look-ing at the same thing."

The man rejoined his girlfriend and I started off again. I chuckled to myself. It was stupid of me to think that somebody would try to take my wallet. Not because there weren't pickpockets around— there were groups that worked this strip regularly— but because they didn't usually target kids. Taking my wallet would mean getting about three bucks, an out-of-date library card, and a couple of bus

was blackjack, roulette, or the slot machines,
u were going to lose in the end. Sure, some peo-
: won for a while, but most lost, and some lost
; . . . really big.

My mother had told me that the dealers and other
or staff were trained to tip off security if somebody
ded up a really big loser. Especially if it was some-
dy who was taking it bad or looked like he couldn't
ord to lose. Security would stay close and even
low him out of the casino and back to his hotel, just
 make sure he was safe. The last thing they wanted
is for a big loser to go to the river and jump in—
mmit suicide.

When my mother first told me that, I said I thought
was pretty decent of them, watching out for these
ys. But she told me that "decent" had nothing to do
th it. Public suicides made for bad publicity, and
it could drive away business. They didn't mind so
ich if some guy killed himself, as long as he did it
ietly—hopefully after he'd left town—so nobody
uld blame the casino.

"Hey, Jay!"

I looked over. My friend Jack was standing at the
en door of one of the video arcades that lined the
eets. He was wearing one of those aprons that hold
ange in a bunch of pockets. Jack worked there.

"How's it going?" I asked.

"Busy. And noisy."

tickets. Not exactly the score t
looking for.

As well, there'd only been him an
Pickpockets usually worked in a tea
least, that's what my mother had to
knew about these things. She was pret
Dan, the head of security at the casin
told me the stories he'd told her.

She said there were teams of thieve
the world, moving from city to cit
thieves, and con men of all differer
work the circuit, from London to N
Atlantic City to Vegas to Niagara Fa
except on a list of casino towns w
Niagara Falls in the same sentence as
sounded like a great way to see the wo
some frequent flier points.

All of the casinos knew about the
tipped each other off. They exchange
and photos and video. Almost every
most casinos was covered by video
security guys did whatever they cou
thieves. They didn't like anybody ri
customers . . . well, anybody who
Not that the casinos ripped peopl
Everything done in the casino was leg
actually cheat anybody. It was just
were always stacked in the casino's fa

The ringing, buzzing, and roaring of a hundred games flooded out through the door. I looked in. The place was packed, and every game seemed to be in use.

"You talk to your boss yet about me working here?" I asked.

"I talked. He said there's no spots right now. Although, to tell you the truth, if he doesn't get off my back and stop giving me so many crappy shifts you might get *my* job."

"You really thinking about quitting?"

"I'm thinking about it all the time. If I could find something else I'd be gone."

"Yeah, jobs are hard to find," I said.

"Maybe for you, because you're only fifteen. I could find another job in ten minutes."

"Then why don't you?"

"What's the point? There are lots of jobs out there, but nothing any better. If I'm gonna do a crappy job I might as well do this one. Besides, I need something that pays more, and that's not so easy to find."

"I didn't know the arcade paid that much."

"I've been here for over a year so I got a raise. I get fifty-five cents an hour over minimum. It's not great, but it's better than I could get starting somewhere else and—"

"I need change!" a kid said as he pushed between Jack and me. He looked to be about ten years old.

"Can't you see we're talking?" Jack asked, sounding irritated.

"I need change . . . now," the kid repeated, practically shoving a five-dollar bill into Jack's face.

I knew Jack, and I knew he wasn't somebody you bothered or pushed around. I had this picture of him giving the kid a backhand—maybe there'd be a job for me then.

Jack snatched the bill away from the kid and stuffed it into his pouch. Then he pulled out a fistful of quarters and started dropping the coins into the kid's outstretched hand.

"Where you from?" Jack asked the kid. He was now smiling and all friendly. That was the last reaction I'd have expected from him.

"New York City," the kid answered.

"Great city you live in. Now enjoy your games, and if you need more change I'm right here."

The kid grunted and disappeared back into the arcade.

"What a rude little puke," I said.

"That's no way to talk about the customers."

"Kid didn't give you a please or a thank-you," I said.

"I should have thanked *him*," Jack said.

"Thanked him for what?"

Jack smiled. "I guess you didn't notice either."

"Notice what?"

"I gave him the change . . . for a *four*-dollar bill."

"There's no such thing as a four-dollar bill."

"Really? Are you sure? He *must* have given me a four-dollar bill because I know for a fact I gave him sixteen quarters."

"Sixteen? You were supposed to give him twenty."

Jack started to laugh. "I know what I should have given him, and if he'd have been polite I would have given him more . . . maybe eighteen quarters."

"You ripped him off," I said. "Way to go."

"I just consider it my little bonus for putting up with people and their crap," Jack said.

"Do you do that all the time?"

Jack leaned in closer. "Not *all* the time, but a lot. Like with that kid, some *tourist* gives me a five-dollar bill and asks for change. I give him back a quarter, maybe two, less than I'm supposed to. Most of the time nobody notices, but if they do I just apologize . . . you know, it was an accident."

Jack laughed, and I laughed along with him.

"My favourites are those foreigners, people from France or Japan who don't speak English any good, or from anyplace where they don't know about our money. They hand me a ten-dollar bill and I give 'em back change for a five. What the hell do they know? Besides, if they can afford to fly halfway around the world to get here they can afford to lose a few bucks."

"It sounds like it could be more than a few bucks."

"Never more than five from any one person, but I just keep track of it and make sure I take out the extra money. Amazing how it adds up!" Jack started laughing again, then stopped himself. He suddenly looked worried. "You won't tell anybody, will you?"

"Come on, man, you should know better than to ask. Just get me a job and show me how to do the same thing."

"You know it. Besides, I only hit the tourists. Never anybody we know."

"Fair is fair," I agreed.

There was an unstated rule that it was okay to take advantage of the tourists. They were only here for a day or so, and usually they had too much money to begin with . . . at least, too much compared to those of us who lived here. You wouldn't do that with somebody you knew, somebody local, but the tourists were fair game.

"You headed over to the power plant?" Jack asked.

"Yeah, how did you know?"

"It sounds like everybody is going there. That's where I'd be if I wasn't working tonight. Have a couple of beers for me, okay?"

"If I don't get there soon I won't even be able to have a couple for *me*. See you later."

"I'm off at one. Maybe I'll see you after that!" Jack yelled out as I started off again.

I hadn't gone more than a dozen feet when I spied somebody else I knew—Kelsey, a girl I used to enjoy talking to in math class. She was behind the glass at the Daredevil Museum, selling tickets. She was busy with a customer and didn't notice me. I hadn't seen her since school ended. She didn't hang out with the kids I hung with, and she never went to any of the bush parties. She did pretty well in school. She seemed nice, too. If she worked to lose a few pounds, and maybe did something about her hair, she wouldn't be half bad-looking. She looked up, saw me, and smiled. She reached her hand out of the little window at the bottom and waved. I waved back. I liked her.

I saw a gap in the traffic and ran across Clifton Hill just as the volcano started its fake eruption once again. Everybody else on the street and people in their cars—including the drivers—turned and gawked. The way they were staring, all open-mouthed and wide-eyed, you'd have thought they were watching the Second Coming of Christ. Fat chance of that. If Christ was coming back to earth, this was the last place he was going to appear. Or maybe it would actually be one of the *first* places. The people here certainly needed his help.

I cut down the alley beside a motel—*Vacancy, Cable TV, Free Movies, Heart-shaped Tubs* the glowing sign advertised. In addition to the gamblers, Niagara Falls still attracted a lot of honeymoon couples, visiting to celebrate their wedding. A couple of friends of my mother worked as maids, though, and they both said the heart-shaped tubs were a pain to clean.

Leaving the alley and Clifton Hill behind was like leaving one world and entering another. The streets here were quiet and much darker. With no neon signs glaring, the only light was from the few scattered street lamps, filtered through the leaves of the trees lining the street on both sides. No one was here. The only signs of life were porch lights, or an occasional voice, or faded music coming out of open windows, or open curtains allowing a glimpse of the life inside. Actually, I liked looking into people's houses as I passed. When it was all light inside and dark on the street you could see them, but they couldn't see you.

I hesitated at the corner, knowing that the route to the right was shorter. I went straight instead. That way I'd pass right by Candice's house. I wanted to go by her place. Maybe because I wanted her father to see me walk by, so he'd know he didn't scare me, that he didn't own the street—that I could walk anyplace I wanted. I'd show him! Then again, what were the odds that he'd even see me? Even if he was sober enough to be standing up, he probably wouldn't be looking out the window. And even if he were, he wouldn't be able to see well enough to know it was me. The only way he could know it was me was if I went up and pounded on his door, and I wasn't about to do that. I wasn't scared, but I wasn't stupid, either.

What I hoped would happen was that Candice would just come out of her house at that instant, just by chance. A coincidence. Or maybe *she'd* see me and then come running out after me. Then I'd say something cool—I wasn't exactly sure what, but maybe something would just come out of my mouth—and then we'd start talking and I'd invite her down to the power plant. I could just picture the look on Timmy's face when I waltzed into the clearing with Candice beside me. I'd offer her a beer and—damn! Would there be any beers left by the time I got there? It was getting later and drier by the minute.

I DUCKED MY HEAD to get through the hole in the high, barbed-wire fence. The fence had been cut open and then patched up dozens of times over the past two years. Finally the power company had decided they were just wasting wire and stopped fixing it. I couldn't figure out why they'd even bothered to begin with. It wasn't like anybody was going to go near the actual power plant. It was a massive cement building that occupied one little piece of land by the river. Most of the property was acres and acres of woods and bush, and that's where we all went to party.

The trees formed a roof overtop of the path, blocking out the stars and moon and making it even darker. I knew the path well. It was straight and smooth, worn down by generations of kids coming out here to party. My mother had once told me that when she was a kid she used to come out here, so she knew what went on. That was why I never told her about my trips to the power plant.

The trail branched out in different directions like little streams from a big river. I could hear voices off to the left and music coming from the right. I hoped Timmy and Bobby had made a fire. I liked sitting around the flames, watching the little embers drifting up and off into the sky, facing the fire and feeling all warm and toasty.

I turned off the main path and toward the spot where we always hung out. It was still some distance away when I started to hear laughter and voices and music. Obviously it wasn't just the two of them. That was both good and bad. More people meant more friends and a better chance that maybe Candice was one of them, but more people also meant there was almost no chance I was getting any beer tonight. I guess that was okay, as long as there was a fire.

Yes, they did have a fire! That was great—especially if I could sit around the fire with Candice! I stopped at the edge of the clearing, just beyond its light. I was only a few feet away, but I was hidden in the darkness, invisible to the people in the clearing I could see so clearly. It was just like looking into people's houses. It felt safe. Nobody could see you, so nobody could judge you—or hurt you.

There were more than a dozen people standing around the fire or sitting on milk crates or logs, staring at the flames and talking and laughing. Lots of people had beer in their hands and there were lots of dead soldiers, empty and overturned beer bottles, littering the ground. Timmy and Bobby were there, of course, but there were other friends, too. Even the people I didn't know, I *knew*. It was a small town, and it seemed like everybody knew you—or knew about you. It was hard to escape people's ideas or expectations in a place like that.

I looked from face to face. Five girls—two of them had their backs to me. One of them did sort of look like—she turned her head slightly to the side—it was Candice! I felt a little jolt of electricity. As that subsided it was replaced by an uneasy feeling in my stomach. Had she been standing at the window watching when her father chased me away, or maybe he had said something to her? What would she think of me now? Did she think I was a loser? Or maybe the fact that she was even there to begin with meant that she thought differently. Had she come because she wanted to see me? That meant that she probably expected me to do something, so I had to put a move on her . . . or did I?

I was still standing there in the dark. Nobody even knew I was there. I could just leave, or I could stay in the shadows, seeing and hearing everything without being seen or heard. I wouldn't have to say or do anything. I'd be free.

I thought back to other times and other places. How many times had I been the new kid in a new school, standing by the fence, by myself, watching as they all stood together and talked and laughed? How many times in how many houses had I watched through the window as kids played on the street? Not so many times that I couldn't have counted if I'd really wanted to, but too many times to even want to recall. Being on the outside looking in was safe in some ways. I stood there looking for a few more seconds. But I didn't want to add one more time to the list—one more time I simply stood on the outside looking in. I took a deep breath to steel myself.

"Hey guys!" I called out as I stepped into the light.

CHAPTER SEVEN

THE PEOPLE I KNEW yelled out a greeting, while a couple who weren't much more than strangers eyed me suspiciously, as if they were wondering whether I belonged there or not. Timmy ended any doubt as he rushed over and gave me a big hug, like I was his long-lost brother. Timmy always got that way when he'd been drinking—probably drinking *my* share of the beer!

"Any beer left?" I demanded as I untangled his arms from around me.

"Course, man! You didn't think we'd leave you dry and not high, did you?"

Timmy staggered back to where he had been sitting. There was a beer case at his feet. He opened it up to reveal one beer sitting among the empties.

"Hey, there's supposed to be more than this left! Who's been taking my beer?" he demanded.

Nobody answered. They were all busy talking, laughing, drinking, and listening to the music blaring out of the boombox sitting on the ground between two of the girls.

I reached into the case and grabbed the beer. I twisted off the cap and took a sip. It wasn't cold anymore, which made the taste even more gross than usual. I couldn't understand how guys said they liked the flavour of beer, or how they could tell one brand from another. It all just tasted like piss to me, and this one was *warm* piss. Still, I tipped back the bottle and started to chug it down.

"Take it easy, man!" Timmy said as he grabbed my arm.

"I don't think *one* beer is going to get me into trouble," I said as I shook off his grip. I put the bottle back up to my mouth and drained it before returning the empty to the case.

"The night is still young," Timmy said. "I'll take care of things for you."

"Like you took care of the beer?"

"I did," he said, leaning in close, his breath stinking of alcohol. "Most of it's safe . . . I've got it right here." He patted his stomach and laughed. "Although maybe some of it needs to escape. Come on." He stood up and pulled me to my feet. "I need to take a leak."

"Congratulations. You can probably do that on your own."

"Probably. Come and talk to me."

He turned and started to walk. I looked over at Candice. She was talking to the girl beside her and wasn't looking at me. I hurried to catch up to Timmy. As I left the clearing, the blackness swallowed me up again and I felt safer.

"Timmy?" I called out.

"Over here."

I startled at his voice. He was only a dozen feet away, but he was invisible to me until he waved his hand. I walked closer but kept some distance to let him have his privacy.

"Man, this feels good," Timmy said. "I was just about to bust a kidney."

"That's what happens when you drink a two-four."

"I didn't drink it all. I shared, including with that Candice girl you like."

"You did?"

"I did." I heard him doing up his zipper and he turned and walked to my side. "I figured your best chance was if she was at least partially drunk. You know, the more she drinks the better you'll look."

"Thanks for the vote of confidence. I still would have liked more than one beer for me," I said.

"And that's why you can have more than one. I stashed two beers."

"You did!"

"I did. Even put 'em where they'd stay cold 'cause I know you don't like 'em warm. Put 'em in that little creek, just by the big rock."

"Thanks, Timmy, I really appreciate it."

"I told ya, I take care of my friends. You should go down and get 'em . . . but not alone. You should take somebody with you."

"Haven't you already had enough to drink?" I asked. I wasn't grateful enough to want to split the last two beers with him.

"Not me, you idiot! Take somebody you want to share things with," he said. "How about, like maybe, that Candice girl? Wouldn't you like to share a few things with her, man?"

I didn't answer.

"Ask if she wants another beer. If she says yes, then the two of you go off to get 'em. Just think, a cold beer, a girl you like, privacy, and darkness. Darkness may be the only thing that makes you look better than alcohol."

"Shut up, Timmy."

"After everything I've done for you, you're telling me to shut up?"

He had been pretty thoughtful. I mumbled an apology.

"That's better. Sounds pretty good, don't it?"

"I don't know."

"What don't you know? You like her, right?"

"I don't really know her."

"Would you like to get to know her?"Timmy asked. "'Cause that would involve you having to talk. So go."

"I will. I'm just waiting for the right moment."

"That moment better be right now before some-body else hits on her."

I spun around to face the clearing. She was still sitting there, talking to that girl. "I don't see anybody. Who's going to hit on her?"

"Me."

"You?"

"Yeah, look at her . . . she's hot."

"I thought we were friends," I gasped.

"We are. And that's why I'm giving you a warning, a head start, and a push all at once. You want her, you go and get her. If you don't, then I'm gonna put a move on her and you can have her friend."

"Her friend? You mean the girl with her?"

Timmy nodded.

"But she's . . . she's . . ."

"Ugly?" Timmy asked.

"I didn't say that."

"But I bet you were thinking it. She's all yours." He paused. "But if you want that Candice girl instead, then you've got the next two minutes. Use it or lose it, man." Timmy smiled. "It's now or never."

We walked back into the light, and I felt open and exposed, like every eye was on me. Every eye, of course, except for Candice's. She hadn't seen me go and she hadn't noticed me return.

"Go on,"Timmy said as he gave me a little push. He went and sat back down while I slowly circled around the fire until I stood in front of Candice, between her and the fire. She was still lost in conversation, unaware I was there until her friend looked up at me. Candice looked up and smiled. Thank goodness she smiled.

"Hey," I said. So much for a brilliant opening line.

"Hey."

"I didn't know you'd be here tonight," I said.

"Me neither . . . I mean, I didn't know you were going to be here, but I knew I was going to be here . . . at least, I didn't know right away but later on . . . you know what I mean."

I nodded. Somehow her being nervous made me feel less nervous.

"Do you want another beer?" I asked.

"I don't think there are any left."

"You have to know where to look. Come on and I'll show you."

She said something to her friend, who giggled, and then she got up. She followed me as I circled back around the fire. Now I wasn't imagining it—everybody *was* looking at us as we walked. I stopped at the top of the path leading away.

"It's this way," I said, and started down the path. She followed.

"It's dark," she said. "I can't really see where I'm going."

"Here." Without thinking I reached back and took her hand . . . wow, that was smooth. Maybe that was the secret: don't think. That would explain why Timmy did so well . . . he never thought about anything.

"I know where I'm going," I said.

"Is it far?" Candice asked.

"Not far."

The path got narrower and I had to walk in front. I still held on to her hand, pulling her along behind me. Was my hand getting sweaty? Maybe she'd think it was her hand.

I stopped in front of the little creek. It wasn't very big—a few little drops that accumulated as it trickled through the forest before plunging down to the river below.

"Why don't you have a seat?" I said, gesturing to a rock. Candice sat down while I knelt and began fishing around in the water. It was cold . . . refreshing. Timmy *had* put the bottles in here, hadn't he? He wouldn't have been just screwing around with my head . . . that would be so embarrassing. My hand knocked against one of the bottles—right where it should be—and then a second one.

"Here we go, Candice," I said as I stood up, brandishing the bottles. I put one down by my feet, twisted the top off the second—a gentleman always took the cap off—and handed it to Candice.

"Thanks," she said. "But you can call me Candy if you want . . . all my friends do."

"Sure . . . okay . . . Candy." That sounded good. I had a sweet tooth and liked Candy.

I grabbed the second, twisted off the cap, and sat down beside her. The rock wasn't very big so I was pressed right up against her. I took a swig of beer to lubricate my throat so I could talk. Cold beer certainly was better than warm.

"I went by your place on the way here," I said.

"You didn't call on me, did you?" she asked anxiously.

"Nah," I said, shaking my head. "I figured you'd probably be gone by the time I got there. Besides, I didn't think your father would be that happy to see me."

"You've got that right, but don't take it personally. He doesn't like any boys calling on me. He says all boys are jerks."

"And most men," I added. "But don't worry about it. It's no big deal."

"It's funny, though," she said. "He *really* doesn't like you."

My stomach did a flip. "I guess you heard what happened."

"I *saw* what happened."

Whatever chance I had of getting with her was now gone. Maybe it would be better to just get up and leave.

"I told him that I thought you were a nice guy," Candice said.

"I *am* a nice guy," I agreed, suddenly feeling better. "It's just that he really doesn't know me."

"But he does know your father. He *hates* him. What's that all about?" Candice asked.

"I don't know."

"Maybe you could ask your father."

"Can't."

"Doesn't he live with you?" she asked.

"He doesn't live with anybody. He's dead."

"I didn't know . . . I'm so sorry."

I took a slug from the bottle. "That's okay. It was a long time ago. I was little."

"How old were you?" she asked.

"Three . . . almost four."

"That's terrible. Do you even remember him?"

I shook my head. How could you remember somebody you'd hardly ever met? I stood up and tipped back the bottle, draining it.

"My father mentioned that your mother was pretty young when she had you," Candice said. "Maybe that's why he doesn't like your father."

"Maybe. She just turned seventeen on the day I was born. We have the same birthday."

"Wow, that is young."

"It is," I agreed. "But if your father and my father went to school at the same time, then your mother couldn't have been that much older when you were born."

"She was in her twenties," Candice said.

"Are you sure?"

Candice nodded her head. "She's thirty-five now so if you subtract my age that would mean that she was . . . she was twenty-two or twenty-three when I was born."

"That can't be right. If she's thirty-five now and she was twenty-three when you were born, then that would make you—"

"I'll be thirteen in two weeks."

I felt like somebody had just kicked me in the head. "You'll be what?"

"I'll be thirteen on July twenty-fourth."

"You're twelve years old?" I gasped. No wonder her father was mad at me—if she was my daughter, I would have been out there with a baseball bat too! She was just a kid!

"Most people think I look older," Candice said. "Do you think I look older?"

"Yeah, of course!" I exclaimed. If I'd known she was twelve there was no way I'd have been out there in the woods all snuggled up to her and thinking about . . . I jumped to my feet.

"I thought you were fifteen, or at least fourteen . . . honestly!" I stammered. "I had no idea you were twelve!"

"Really I'm thirteen, almost, and people tell me I look older than fifteen. Last month when I was out at a restaurant and the waitress thought I was old enough to drink . . . isn't that funny?"

"Yeah, funny." I looked at the beer in her hand. "You shouldn't be drinking!" I grabbed the bottle.

"What are you doing?" she demanded as she jumped to her feet.

"You're only twelve! You shouldn't be drinking!"

"I've been drinking for a long time!" she exclaimed. "Over two months!" She reached for the bottle and I pulled it away so she couldn't get it.

"Give me back my beer!"

"You can't have it!" I turned around and tossed the beer into the trees. I heard the bottle smash.

"What are you, some sort of psycho?" she demanded. "That was my beer!"

"It was my beer, and you shouldn't have had any of it! Go!" I shouted. "Go back to the clearing, now!"

"You can't order me around!" she snapped, putting her hands on her hips.

"Fine . . . stay here if you want, but I'm leaving." I started walking away in the opposite direction from the clearing.

"Where are you going?" she yelled.

I turned around. "Can you find your way back to the clearing?"

"Yeah."

"Then you'd better do that." I turned and started to walk away again. She kept yelling at me. I didn't turn. I didn't answer. I kept walking toward the gorge.

CHAPTER EIGHT

I SAT ON THE LEDGE, my legs dangling over. Down through my feet—far below my feet—I could see the river. It was still dark so I couldn't see things clearly, but I could catch glimmering glimpses of the water. I figured it was at least a twenty-metre drop into the rapids. The water twisted and roared and raged as it raced over and between the rocks that dotted the river. A drop from there would probably be deadly. Maybe it wouldn't. It would depend on where you fell, whether you hit rock or water, and how deep the water was if you did hit it. Even if the drop didn't kill you, what came next probably would. The current would sweep you in one of two directions. Either you'd be caught up in the water-intake for the power plant and crushed in the generators— or you'd go over the Falls.

Of course there was a chance you might be able to drag yourself to shore first, or cling to a rock and wait for daybreak, when somebody would see you and

send out a rescue team. You could drop into the water
and live. It *could* happen.

I'd even seen it happen before. There were these
three guys fishing on the river one day, upstream.
Their engine died and the boat started drifting
toward the Falls. It got caught up in the current,
going faster and faster as it got closer and closer.
Somehow—dumb luck, I guess—it got wedged
between two rocks.

I watched—almost everybody in Niagara Falls
was watching—as a Coast Guard helicopter hov-
ered overtop of them. Then the door opened and a
guy appeared, and he went over the side attached to
a rope, like a spider on a thread, and dropped down
onto that boat. One by one the men on the boat
were pulled up to the helicopter. I could have
sworn that I saw that boat wobble and shift as each
man was lifted off. Finally the rescuer was pulled up
and the helicopter flew away. That guy had to be the
bravest guy I ever saw in my whole life. I saw him
interviewed on TV. He was a search-and-rescue
expert with the Coast Guard. He talked about
how it was a little tricky but all "part of the job."
What a job!

Funny, I'd thought that boat was going to be swept
away any second. But that was two years ago, and the
remains of the boat were still there, stuck on those
rocks.

I knew a lot of people were afraid of heights, didn't like going right to the edge, but not me. Looking down into the swirling water below my dangling feet, I almost felt like taking the drop myself, right there and then, rushing over the edge with the force of the rapids, if only to get the hell out of there. Away from all the stupid, loser things I'd said and done and all the people who thought they knew me. Sitting there I could feel the Falls pulling hard at me, and I understood why some people actually wanted to end it all that way. But I figured I needed to be a lot more drunk, or maybe it wasn't my time. Besides, with my luck, I figured I'd just end up stuck on the rocks, like that boat, something new for the tourists to gawk at.

"I figured I'd find you here."

I turned around. It was Timmy.

"What are you doing?" he asked.

"Sitting."

"I see that. Why are you sitting *here* instead of around the fire?"

"Better view here. See for yourself," I said as I patted the space beside me.

"No way, man. Why don't you come back to the fire?"

"Told you. I like the view here better."

Timmy slumped to the ground behind me, away from the edge. "I take it things didn't go so well with Candice."

"They didn't go bad."

"And that's why she's back at the fire and you're here by yourself."

"I'm where I want to be," I said.

He shook his head. "I don't know why you like it here so much. Heights make my stomach go all weird and my knees buckle. Doesn't it bother you at all?"

"I like high places."

"The only high I like involves a bottle,"Timmy said. "You want something else to drink?"

"Like I have a choice."

Timmy reached into his jacket and pulled something out. "Ta-dah!"

"What is it?"

"Something special. Amaretto."

"What?"

"Come here and see for yourself."

It was pretty obvious what he was doing—trying to get me off the rock—but I didn't care. I'd sat there long enough anyway, and the beer I'd had really wasn't enough, all things considered. I took one more look through my legs to the river below then got up and walked over to Timmy. He stood up and handed me the bottle. It was square-shaped, with a big fancy label.

"It's a liqueur. Try it."

I twisted off the cap. It was big and square, just like the bottle. I smelled the stuff. It was sweet—almost sickly sweet. I tipped the bottle and took a taste. The booze was even sweeter than its smell, and thick.

"Here, let me have a slug," Timmy said as he took the bottle. He took a big gulp. "It's like drinking liquid candy."

"More like drinking maple syrup."

"Maple syrup with a kick. Do you know how much alcohol is in this stuff?"

"More than beer?"

"Way more. *Way* more."

I took the bottle from Timmy and took another drink. This time it wasn't just a sip. I tipped the bottle back and took a long, long drink. It did taste like candy . . . the only candy I was going to get that night.

CHAPTER NINE

I ROLLED OVER and the bright light pierced my eyes, sending spears of pain deep into my brain. I closed my eyes tight and brought my hand up to shield them from the light. Why was it so bright in here . . . in my bedroom. My bedroom? How did I get here? What happened?

I tried to sit up and my stomach lurched and I knew I was going to throw up. My guts heaved violently but nothing came out except a little bit of foam and saliva. I looked down on the floor. There was a puddle of puke already there. My stomach lurched badly again and I gagged, but nothing came out. There was probably nothing left to come out. My stomach was empty because I'd emptied it earlier on. When, I didn't remember. I didn't remember much. There was me and Timmy and the bottle, and then we went back to the fire and . . . I remembered saying some stupid things . . . and then nothing. I didn't know how I'd got home. What time was it?

Slowly, hesitantly, I climbed out of bed. My legs felt shaky. My stomach did a flip again, but finally settled down. My head hurt . . . the whole thing was throbbing, but the left temple really hurt. The whole world seemed to be on a tilt. I looked down. I was wearing one shoe while the other foot was bare, not even a sock. I put a hand against the dresser to steady myself.

My head was really hurting. I couldn't believe how much. I put my hand up to the spot on my head that hurt the most. It felt raw and painful to the touch. I drew away my hand. There was a little bit of blood! I staggered toward the mirror on my door and—

"Aaah!"

I'd stepped into the puke with my bare foot! I lifted up my foot and almost fell over, so I ended up putting my foot back down into the puddle and my foot slipped out from under me and I almost tumbled into the puke.

I limped over and leaned against the dresser again. I reached down and grabbed a shirt off the floor and wiped the puke off my foot. With one foot off the ground I almost tumbled over again. I teetered, regained my balance, and tossed the shirt into the corner. As I put my foot back down I realized I hadn't gotten all of the puke off. I could feel it squishing between my toes. What did it matter? I was going to have to have a shower anyway. I kicked off my other shoe.

I looked into the mirror and was shocked by the image staring back. The whole left side of my face was covered in dried blood! I felt around. There was still a sore, raw spot in my scalp, hidden beneath matted, bloody hair. There was no way I could tell how big the cut was. I knew, from experience, that cuts to the head really bled a lot, even if the cut wasn't that bad. Besides, it had almost stopped bleeding on its own, so how bad could it be?

I put my ear close to the door and listened. There was no sound. Was my mother still asleep? Had I gotten in before her last night? Did she know anything? And if she didn't know, could I clean everything up and cover it up so she never would?

The cut on my head could probably be explained away. After all, how many times had I cut or bruised or broken something, doing something I shouldn't have done? Between bikes, mini-bikes, my go-kart, and doing stuff that was just plain stupid, I'd gotten hurt a lot. I'd broken my left arm twice, trying to do the same thing two different times.

When we lived in Welland—one of the times we lived in Welland—the house we rented was across an alley from the house where one of my friends lived. The two houses were only separated by that one little alley. A narrow alley. I figured I could jump from the roof of my house to the roof of his house. I didn't make it. And it was a lot farther down than it was across. That was how I broke my arm the first time.

My mother couldn't believe I'd broken my arm trying to jump between houses. But she *really* didn't believe it when, the day after the cast came off, I did it again, missed again, and broke the same arm, again. At least it was in a different place. Someday I wanted to go back there and do it a third time ... not the breaking-the-arm part, but the jump. Except this time I'd make it.

I opened the door a crack. Bright sunshine flooded into my brain with a sharp jab. I stifled an urge to cry out in pain. Shielding my eyes, I tiptoed down the hall and into the bathroom, locking the door behind me.

I peeled off my remaining sock, one hand against the wall to support my faulty balance. I pulled my T-shirt over my head. It was sticky and smelled foul—like alcohol, sweat, and vomit. I dropped it to the floor. I'd do a whole load of laundry, including this shirt and the one I'd used to wipe off my foot. Next I unbuckled my pants and let them drop to the floor. I stepped out of them and then removed my boxers.

I turned on the taps. The water splashed out, cold, with a brown tinge, which was how it always looked when the taps were first turned on. I adjusted the taps, waiting for the water from the old hot-water heater in the basement to make its way up through the pipes to the bathroom. It got less cold and then warm and finally hot. I climbed into the tub and pulled the shower curtain so it completely circled and surrounded me.

The stream of water felt so good. I shampooed my hair, delicately probing my scalp with my fingers to find the wound. The shampoo stung the wound slightly but the hurt almost felt good. I stuck my head back under the flow of water, washing away the suds and vomit and who knew what.

Next I soaped up my whole body. I didn't want to miss a spot. I wanted to wash away whatever had happened last night. What exactly *had* happened last night?

It was scary to think that I couldn't remember, that I'd lost a night, or at least part of a night. Maybe it was better that way, or maybe it wasn't. Either way, I was sure Timmy would tell me all about it. Assuming *he* could remember.

I turned the shower off and grabbed a towel. I felt cleaner but not much better. I could wash away the blood from my hair but not the throbbing in my head. My stomach lurched again. Maybe I was just hungry and I should eat. Then again, that might be a big mistake. Food in the stomach was just something else to throw up.

I wrapped the towel around my waist and bundled up all my clothes. I unlocked the door and quickly crossed over to my room, closing the door behind me. I dropped the clothes to the floor and kicked them into

the corner to join the pile of dirty clothes that had accumulated there. When my mother headed to work I'd do
the laundry—my clothes as well as hers. I knew how to
do it. There were lots of things that I'd had to learn to
do for myself over the years when she was too drunk to
do a lot of the things that a parent would usually do.

Quickly I pulled on new clothes. I really was hungry.
I was going to have to risk eating. I went down the stairs,
the old wooden steps creaking underfoot. Halfway
down I heard sounds coming from the kitchen—a radio
and plates rattling. Obviously my mother was
awake. She turned around as I entered the room.

"Good morning," I said, trying to sound chipper. It
seemed awfully bright in there.

"It's barely morning," she said, gesturing up at the
clock. It was eleven-thirty. "And I'm not sure how
good it is, either."

She knew something. *How much?* was the question.
I sat down at the table.

"How is your head?" my mother asked.

"My head? It's not bad . . . it's nothing . . . just a
little cut."

"I know it's cut—remember I practically carried
you inside—I just want to know how badly is it cut?
It had stopped bleeding before I put you to bed."

"It's nothing," I repeated as she rushed over. "I fell
down, tripped on a crack in the sidewalk, really
stupid, but I'm okay."

She moved my hair so she could try to find the cut. I jumped as she located it, with her fingernail!

"Be careful!" I pleaded.

"It isn't me who should be careful."

"Accidents happen," I said. "I tripped." I probably had tripped.

"I guess that happens to people who are *drunk*."

I felt a shiver go up my spine. Obviously she knew everything. Or at least she *thought* she knew everything.

"I wasn't drunk."

She snorted.

"So I had something to drink. That doesn't mean I was drunk." A partial truth was the best lie.

"You were drunk. Don't forget, you're talking to an expert."

"On drinking or being drunk?"

"On *both*." She reached over and grabbed a cigarette from the package on the counter.

"I thought you were stopping again last night," I chided her, trying to shift the conversation away from me.

"I did stop again last night." She struck a match and lit the cigarette, inhaling and then letting out a cloud of bluish smoke. "I started again just after I found my son on the front steps of the house, unconscious, bleeding, and lying in a pool of vomit."

I felt my stomach pitch again and tried not to show it. I tried not to show anything. Obviously she knew everything. She might even know more than I knew. Lying was hard when you didn't even have any idea what the truth was.

"Do you know where your other shoe is?" she asked.

I shook my head.

"Those were expensive shoes. Weren't they your favourites?"

I nodded.

"We're not made of money. I don't have another two hundred dollars to go throwing away on another pair of ..." She stopped. "Listen to me. Talking about the shoes instead of what really matters. I sound like *my* mother."

"So what happens now?" I asked.

"What happens is that we try to get some food into you."

"I'm not sure that's such a good idea," I said.

"Something bland. Unbuttered toast or some dry cereal. Cheerios always worked for me. This may be the one time that having an alcoholic for a mother works in your favour, because I know the drill."

She went over to the cupboard and pulled out a box of Cheerios. She put it down on the counter and reached farther into the back and pulled out another box of Cheerios—a brand new box—and opened it. She poured a little into a bowl and brought it over and set it down in front of me.

"Fresh Cheerios are better when you're not putting milk on them. Use your fingers. Just take them a couple at a time. If it's not feeling good then stop eating." She walked over, opened the cupboard under the sink, and pulled out a bucket. "And if you need to throw up again, try to use this instead of the floor," she said as she put it down beside me. "After you eat and we talk, you should go back to bed."

"I'd like to go back to bed and . . . what are we going to talk about?"

She scowled. "What do you *think* we're going to talk about?"

I knew. I just needed to ask.

"I probably should have had this conversation with you a long time ago. I figured it was coming but I just hoped it wouldn't."

"You figured this was coming?" I asked.

"I work in a casino. I know all about odds. And the odds were that you and I would have to have a conversation about alcohol."

"We've had *hundreds* of conversations about alcohol," I pointed out.

"I guess we didn't have the right conversation," my mother said. "I need to talk to you about blood."

"Blood? Am I bleeding again?" I asked as I reached up to my head.

"I'm not talking about what's coming out of you. I'm talking about what you have running through your veins."

"What does that mean?"

"Alcoholism is in your genes."

"There's nothing in my jeans except a few bucks," I said, trying to make a joke.

"Don't be funny. It's a genetic trait. If there's a family history of alcoholism it's more likely that a child will become an alcoholic when they grow up."

"What are you saying?" I demanded, although it was pretty obvious what she was getting at.

"The odds are increased if you have an alcoholic parent."

"'Odds' doesn't mean for sure. Not everybody whose mother is an alcoholic becomes an alcoholic."

"A predisposition to alcoholism is inherited."

"So is eye colour, but my eyes are blue and yours are brown."

"The same colour as your father's eyes," she said.

I hesitated. We never talked about him, hardly ever mentioned him. And the few times he did come up I always said "he" or "him." Words like "father" and "Dad" seemed like they were from a foreign language that my mouth couldn't quite pronounce.

"I didn't know that he had blue eyes."

"He did. Beautiful blue eyes. He also had serious problems with alcohol, although he never admitted it. You have bad blood coming from both sides." She paused and looked away for a few seconds, like she was seeing something in the distance. She turned back. "At least your father was a friendly drunk. Not like his father, your grandfather."

"His old man was a drunk?"

"He was awful. Loud, obnoxious, stood on the street corner yelling at people, swearing, picking fights with strangers. He'd keep that up until he eventually fell down dead drunk."

"He sounds like an idiot."

"It was when he was drinking. Watching it was bad enough, but to have to live with it in the same house would have been . . . would have been . . . unbelievable."

I knew what it was like to live with an alcoholic, but my mother was never awful. She was just sort of not there, or not all there. She'd pass out, or not come home when she was supposed to, or I'd have to fix my own meal—and feed her as well—or do the laundry myself.

"Your grandfather was a big man and a mean drunk. He was abusive. I remember seeing your grandmother—your father's mother—with bruises and black eyes."

"Somebody should have called the cops on him," I said.

"You have to remember it was different back then. Lots of people just pretended they didn't see it. And others saw it but figured they had no right to interfere or were afraid to step in—like I said, your grandfather was mean and big."

"If anybody hit *you* it wouldn't matter how big they were," I said. "I'd find a way to take them down."

"And nobody ever has hit me. My father was always pretty gentle, and maybe some of my boyfriends haven't been the best, but nobody's ever hit me."

"Nobody should ever hit a woman," I said.

She smiled. "That's something else you share with your father, as well as eye colour. He started stepping in to protect his mother, so every time your grandfather aimed his anger at her your father got between them. He took it on, until all the abuse was coming at him. It was awful," she said, shaking her head, "and I had a front-row seat for all of it."

"You saw it happen?"

"Mostly just the results. The bruises."

"You knew him back then . . . when he was a kid?"

"Practically since I was born. He grew up down the street."

"*This* street?"

"You know this is where I was raised."

"Yeah. I just didn't know *he* was raised here . . . I only knew it was somewhere here in the Falls."

"Right here. Five doors down."

"Down?" I questioned, gesturing down the street. "There are only two other houses down before the parking lot."

"It's a parking lot now, but not then. His mother and my mother were good friends. I guess I didn't mention any of this to you."

What was to guess? She'd never mentioned anything to me. I knew hardly anything about him.

"I always thought you'd be more curious about your father," she said.

I shrugged. There were things that I wanted to know, things she should have told me that she hadn't, but there never seemed to be a right time to ask.

"Do you have questions?" she asked.

What should I say? What questions could I ask? There was so much.

"Well? There must be something about him you'd like to know, isn't there?"

I started to answer when my stomach did a flip. I ran from the room, reaching the bathroom just in time to throw up the Cheerios into the toilet.

CHAPTER TEN

I SNEAKED TO THE BACK DOOR. I didn't want to talk to my mother anymore. I'd done all the talking with her I wanted to do for one day. Now I needed to talk to Timmy.

"I'm goin' out!" I yelled, slamming the door closed behind me before my mother could answer. I trotted down the street, trying to put some distance between the house and me. My legs felt better, but they were still a little wobbly. I turned through the parking lot and came to a stop. Partly because I was out of sight of my house. Partly because I felt winded. Partly just to think. I was standing right about where his house used to be.

I tried to imagine the house that used to be there. I assumed it would have looked a lot like the rest of the places on the street. I could picture the rooms, even the furniture in the rooms. What I couldn't picture was him. I hadn't seen a picture since I was little. My mother had some pictures. At least, I figured she still had them. I remembered looking at them but I couldn't remember him, really. He had blue eyes like mine. I knew that now. I closed my eyes and pictured a pair of blue eyes staring back. Eyes that looked like mine, looking back at me, like I was staring into a mirror. But I couldn't picture much else.

There was a leather jacket—he wore a leather jacket. That's what Candice's old man had said. And he was probably big. His father was big, and I was big for my age, so that had to make sense. My father was probably a big guy.

I opened my eyes. That wasn't much of a picture. More gaps than glimpses. Sort of like last night. Last night I could do something about. I started walking again. Talking to Timmy might at least close one gap.

I came up to the Donut Hole. I peered in through the window, checking the booth that Timmy liked in the back, and then scanning the other booths and the stools at the counter. He wasn't there, but a couple of guys I knew saw me and waved. I waved back. Neither of them had been out at the power plant last night— so far as I could remember—so they wouldn't be able to help fill in the blank spots.

There had to be at least a dozen different places Timmy could be, including his house. I looked at my watch. It was almost three in the afternoon. The house was probably the last place to look. Timmy slept in till noon sometimes, especially after a night that went as long as I figured the night before had gone, but then he always cleared out as soon as he got up. Maybe I should start at the arcade or the—

"Hey, Jay!"

I turned around. It was Timmy! He was waving his hands over his head. He ran across the street, barely dodging cars filled with tourists. One of the cars slowed down, changed lanes, and honked at him. Timmy blew a kiss and then gave them the finger.

"I've been looking for you," I said.

"You would have found me a minute ago if you'd stayed home."

"You were at my place?"

"Just came from there. Your mother didn't seem to be her usual cheerful self." He paused. "Matter of fact, she acted real ticked off."

"She is. That's why I left."

"Welcome to the club."

"I guess I can't blame her," I said. "Coming home drunk, covered in puke and missing a shoe."

"Your shoe, that's right. It's at my house."

"My other shoe is at your house?"

He nodded his head.

"Why do you have my shoe?" I asked.

"Because you gave it to me."

"Why would I give you my shoe?"

Timmy laughed. "You know, you were pretty drunk."

"That's about the only part I do know for sure. But why would I give you my shoe?"

"You said I was like your brother, and since I'd shared my great gift of alcohol with you, you wanted to share your greatest possession with me—your shoes."

"Come on."

"You made a really big speech. And then you decided it would be better to just give me one shoe and you'd keep the other. You said instead of blood brothers we'd be Nike brothers."

"Man, I don't remember any of that."

Timmy started to laugh. "Then I guess you don't remember picking a fight with a couple of the guys."

"I picked a fight?"

"Two fights. One with Tommy and the other with Justin."

"But those are my friends. Why would I pick a fight with them?"

"You thought they were trying to pick up Candice," Timmy said. "You started yelling at them, telling them that she was *only a child* and—"

"She *is* only a child. She's only twelve!"

"Yeah, I know. Everybody knows. You kept telling everybody at the top of your lungs."

"I can't remember any of that," I said, shaking my head.

"And then you threatened to fight people—every-body—including all the girls, and you started to call people perverts and child molesters for even think-ing about being with her." Timmy paused. "Although I thought that was pretty funny, because didn't *you* want to be with her?"

"Before I found out how young she is!" I protested. "It sounds like it got really ugly. Did I actually fight anybody?"

"I wouldn't call it a fight. One shot and you went down like a sack of potatoes."

"Was it Justin who hit me?" I asked. He was a year older and big—real big. One shot from him would have practically put down a bear.

"No, Justin wouldn't hit you. He's your friend."

"It was Tommy?" Tommy was my age, but so skinny that a good wind could have blown him away.

"Tommy? Tommy never hits anybody."

"Then if it wasn't Justin and it wasn't Tommy, who hit me?"

Timmy started to chuckle.

"I'm glad you think this is so funny. Who hit me?"

"Candice."

"Candice? Candice hit me?"

"She kept telling you to shut up but you wouldn't listen. You kept going on and on and on, telling every-body she was a kid and not to give her alcohol or touch her or anything."

"I was drunk."

"Yeah, I think we all know that. So finally she jumps to her feet and gives you a shot to the head and down you go."

"No way. No way could she hit me that hard. My head is all cut up."

"She was holding a rock. She hit you with it." Timmy started laughing some more, like he was watching it happen again. Maybe if it hadn't been me I would have thought it was funny too.

"And then she stood over you, swearing and spitting. She even tried to kick you but Justin held her back."

"I guess I should thank Justin."

"You should. If it wasn't for him you would have had the crap beaten out of you by a girl . . . a twelve-year-old girl."

"Thanks for pointing that out. At least that explains why I can't remember anything."

"What do you mean?" Timmy asked.

"You know, because I got knocked out."

"No you didn't. You got back to your feet, blood all over your face, and started yelling at Justin because you thought he was hugging Candice when he was just holding her back."

"This gets worse and worse."

"It would have, if I hadn't gotten you out of there. That's when I took you home. Me and Tommy."

"Yeah. Haven't you ever felt that way?"

"No way. My father expects the worst of me and I hardly ever let him down. I always set the bar so low that if I ever make a mistake and *don't* screw up he'll be surprised and shocked. That's the secret."

"Not much of a secret."

Timmy shrugged. "Works for me."

"I better get going. I'll give you a call tomorrow."

I sat down on the curb and Timmy sat d[...]
me. I didn't know what to say. It would hav[...]
ter not to have known any of that. It would[...]
better for nobody to have known, but I fig[...]
probably the talk of the town by now.

"Don't sweat it," Timmy said. "It's no bi[...]

"No big deal?" I couldn't believe my ear[...]

"You got drunk and you got stupid an[...]
beaten up by a twelve-year-old girl. So wh[...]
be a lot worse."

"It could? How?" I asked.

"She could have been ten years old." [...]
"Or even worse, it could have been *me* she[...]

Timmy was laughing so hard now I co[...]
laughing along with him.

"So, what are we going to do tonight?" [...]

"I don't know what you're going to d[...]
going to be staying home."

"Did your mother ground you?"

I shook my head. "She didn't do anyth[...]
she'd yelled at me or punished me or d[...]
thing."

"You *want* to get punished? Just how ha[...]
girl hit you?"

"Not hard enough. It was just the way [...]
looked at me. She wasn't mad as much as s[...]
I don't know . . . disappointed."

"Disappointed?"

CHAPTER ELEVEN

I CAME INTO THE HOUSE as quietly as possible, and the house was as quiet as me. There was no TV or radio. No voices. Maybe my mother was out, or maybe she was just having a nap. She'd gotten into the habit of taking an afternoon nap when she pulled a late shift, and now she took one most days, even when she wasn't working. It was so quiet that I could hear the clock ticking from the other room. I couldn't remember ever hearing that before. I usually came in with a lot of noise and then threw on the TV or radio or my CD player. I liked background noise. It made it seem like I wasn't alone in the house . . . was I alone now?

I opened the cupboard under the sink and grabbed a bag of potatoes. I pulled out five and put them in the sink. I wasn't completely sure what I was going to make for supper but I knew it would involve potatoes—it always involved potatoes. I took the peeler out of the drawer and started peeling.

It was strange. Usually I looked forward to the days my mother was off work, but today I wanted some more time to pass before I saw her again. I didn't want to talk about what had happened anymore— although there were things that still needed to be said. Actually, I didn't know which was worse, talking about difficult things or being in the same room and leaving them alive but unspoken.

We used to have tons of times like that back when my mother was drinking. It was like having an elephant in the room. Nobody wanted to talk about it, and we both just hoped it would get up and leave by itself—or at least not trample us. There were lots of things we were both thinking but neither of us mentioned. Things like where she'd been when she'd left me alone all night. Why there was no money for a school field trip but there was money for booze. Why the fridge could be empty except for a new twelve-pack of beer. Things like me finding her passed out on the floor and helping get her into bed. Like the TV or stereo or some of my toys suddenly disappearing while I was at school. Like us having to disappear in the middle of the night, throwing our stuff in the back of a truck, helped by men I didn't know and would never see again. Just like I'd never see the kids I'd played with, or my school, or what I'd left behind in my desk, or the friends I'd made, or . . . a shudder went through my entire body.

Maybe the elephant had left the room but I could still clearly picture it.

I hadn't thought about not thinking about things in a long time.

It was five years since my mother had stopped drinking, so it was maybe three years since I hadn't worried every single day. Now it was just some days, or really only little parts of some days. Even then, when the worry did creep in, I didn't always know what it was about right away.

The worry would start as a tiny spot in the back of my brain and then it would start to spread. Had I locked the front door when I left? Had I turned off the burner on the stove? Was the toaster unplugged? Was there some assignment at school that was due today? It was like knowing that something was wrong but not being able to put my finger on it. And that feeling got bigger and bigger until there was no spot that it didn't fill. It was like a buzzing that got louder and louder and louder.

Lots of times the worrying was about my mother. Worrying about her became a habit. Where was she, was she okay, was she in trouble? Actually, where was she now? Was she sleeping?

I had to go upstairs to gather the dirty clothes to put in a load of laundry. I could check on her then, see if she was asleep. I really needed to do all that laundry. There was no point in putting it off. The sooner it was done, the quicker another piece of evidence would be eliminated.

I finished the last of the potatoes. I put the stopper in the sink and ran cold water so they were covered. I rinsed off my hands and dried them on my T-shirt. Another item for the laundry.

I turned around then and saw it. There was a bottle of alcohol sitting in the middle of the kitchen table! I froze, except for the hairs on the back of my neck, which all stood up. I stared at it. Big red letters on the bottle. Vodka. A bottle of vodka. The top was on but I could see it was half empty. Half gone. Half drunk.

I felt numb. This wasn't possible. There had to be a mistake. I wasn't really seeing what I was seeing. Slowly I walked over to the table, keeping my eyes fixed on the bottle, like it would disappear or run off if I looked away. I picked it up. Feeling it in my hand— the cold, smooth glass—made it real. I unscrewed the cap and brought the bottle up to my face. The fumes that stung my nose left no doubt it was alcohol.

That feeling in my brain buzzed to life, flashing from the one spot to fill my entire head. I wasn't just anxious or worried, I felt completely panicked. My whole body flushed. Where was my mother? I set the bottle down on the table.

"Mom!" I screamed as I ran from the kitchen. "Mom, where are you!" I yelled as I raced up the stairs and threw open her bedroom door. Her bed was unmade but empty. Where was she? Was she lying somewhere . . . unconscious? I ran back down the stairs, yelling as I ran, "Mom! Mom . . . where are you?"

"Jay!"

I ran toward her voice, bursting back in through the kitchen door as she came running up the basement stairs. I threw my arms around her.

"Jay, what's wrong? What's wrong?" she exclaimed.

"I didn't know where you were . . . I was worried," I sobbed, tears coming to my eyes.

"I was just in the basement . . . You're crying!"

"I'm not crying," I said, as I reached up and brushed away the tears I didn't want to admit to.

"What's wrong . . . what's wrong?"

"The bottle ... on the table."

"I shouldn't have left it there. I didn't want you to see it."

"You're worried about me *seeing* it? Maybe you just shouldn't have *drunk* it!" I shouted as I released her and stepped back. My tears had been burned away by a burst of anger. "How could you do it? How could you start drinking again?"

"I wasn't drinking."

"Don't lie to me!" I snapped.

"I'm not lying."

"The proof is right there!" I said, pointing at the table. I had the urge to reach over and grab it, smash the bottle on the ground or throw it at her. "It's half empty! Are you going to tell me the vodka just evaporated?"

"No, I drank it."

"So you admit it!"

"I drank it five years ago."

"What? What are you talking about?"

She walked over and picked up the bottle. "This is the last bottle of alcohol I ever drank from."

"I don't understand."

"Five years ago I drank twenty ounces before I quit. That was the last time I drank."

"And you kept the bottle?" I asked, incredulous.

She nodded.

"But that doesn't make any sense. Why didn't you throw it away?"

"Because this bottle is important to me."

"Yeah, right. If the bottle is so important, then why didn't you just pour the vodka down the drain and keep the bottle?" I asked. What sort of lie was she trying to sell me?

"Because the alcohol is just as important."

"More important than *me*, obviously."

"It *was* more important. I haven't been drinking. Not for five years. You know that."

"Do I? You still haven't explained that bottle!"

"I'm trying. Sit down and I'll explain everything."

I folded my arms across my chest but didn't move.

"Please?" she asked. She sat down and pushed out a chair for me. Reluctantly I sat.

"I haven't been drinking."

I glared at her but didn't answer.

"Honestly. Do I look as though I'm impaired? Can you smell any alcohol on my breath?"

I looked at her, but in a different way. She didn't look drunk. There was no smell of alcohol.

"I usually keep the bottle right up there over the fridge," she said, gesturing to a cupboard.

"I don't want to know *where* you keep it, I want to know *why* you keep it." My angry feelings were starting to fade.

"I keep it to remind me."

"Remind you of what?"

"That I'm an alcoholic."

"And you need that bottle to remind you of that?"

"I need it to remind me of the last time I drank. Of my commitment not to drink anymore."

"Still, if it's the bottle that's so important, why didn't you pour the vodka down the sink and keep the empty bottle?"

"Because the alcohol is important too."

"Alcohol is always important to an alcoholic!" I said. More important than anything or *anybody* else, I thought, but didn't say.

"And because I will always be an alcoholic, I've kept the alcohol close at hand."

"That doesn't make any sense. Because you're an alcoholic you should never have any alcohol around!"

She chuckled. What was so funny about any of this?

"If there wasn't any alcohol in the house and I wanted some, do you think I couldn't figure out how to get it? There are two beer stores, a liquor outlet, at least three places that sell wine, and a dozen bars within a ten-minute drive of our house."

I didn't like the way she had all that figured out. Had she been drinking at those places? Had she fallen off the wagon and been hiding it from me?

"Not to mention the fact that I work in a casino, where alcohol flows more freely than water."

"Still … why would you keep a bottle here?"

"It's hard to explain."

"Try," I said. I still didn't believe her completely. I leaned forward and tried to smell alcohol on her once again. Nothing.

She didn't answer right away. She was looking down at her hands folded in front of her on the table. She looked up. "I didn't like to worry you."

I laughed out loud.

"I mean not anymore. I know you worry. I just don't want to worry you any more than I have to. I've been dry for five years. You have to believe me. But there have been times when I haven't felt so strong. When your grandfather died. When relationships haven't gone the way I wanted. This morning."

"This morning?"

She nodded. "After you left I just started thinking about alcohol and if you'd be able to escape its clutches."

"There's nothing to escape," I said, feeling a new wave of guilt. "And don't say anything about denial. I'm not denying anything, because there's nothing to deny! And besides, we're talking about you and that bottle!"

She looked as though she was about to say something, but she didn't. "When I'm feeling bad, low, I take out that bottle and I take out a glass."

I noticed for the first time that there was a glass on the table as well.

"And I sit there and I look at the bottle. Sometimes I even take off the cap. And then I have to decide if I'm stronger than that bottle. And so far, every time—with the help of AA and my faith and my friends, and, most important, you—I've been stronger than any bottle and any alcohol." She paused. "I hope you believe me."

I did. It kind of made sense to me when I imagined her doing that. I nodded.

She stood up with the bottle and walked over to the cupboard. Then she opened it and reached up and put the bottle at the very back before closing it.

"There, that's where it'll stay. Maybe there won't be a next time for me to stare that bottle down. But maybe there will be, and I'll know where it's at. And so will you."

"What do you mean?" I asked.

"We both know what I mean."

I felt a tingle of electrical impulses course up my spine.

"Would you like to know why I was in the basement?"

I shrugged.

"I was looking for pictures."

"Pictures of what?"

"Pictures I can show you when I tell you about your father."

CHAPTER TWELVE

FOR THE SECOND TIME in just a few minutes I felt a flush spread over my whole body.

"You do want to hear about him, don't you?"

I did and I didn't. I nodded my head ever so slightly.

"Come on."

She went down the basement stairs. I followed. The stairs were steep and wooden and shaky. The staircase was open on one side except for a thin, wobbly handrail. The steps creaked beneath me. I stopped halfway down.

The basement was piled high with boxes and crates and old chesterfields and broken chairs and years and years of assorted junk that nobody wanted but nobody had the heart or the back to throw out. There were things that my grandparents had accumulated in the years they'd lived here, and then some of our stuff layered on top. Some of the piles were so high that they almost reached to the ceiling—not that the ceiling was very high. There were places where I had to bend down to pass under the beams. There were pipes and wires strung along the ceiling. The only light was from a few bare bulbs hanging down from those beams—and one of those bulbs was burned out. The whole basement smelled bad—a dusty, musty smell. It was so strong that you could almost taste it.

In the centre sat the furnace—big and black, with pipes reaching out of it, spreading and stretching across the basement to reach everywhere in the whole house. It reminded me of a tree. Or an octopus. Or a monster, ready to reach out with those long arms and grab me and stuff me into its grated mouth. During the winter months it was alive. It grunted and groaned, and when it came on there was a glowing, crackling light that leaked out through the grate—through its mouth. I knew it was stupid and I was too old to have thoughts like that . . . but still.

I hardly ever went down there, and never on my own. I was grateful that the washer and the dryer were up on the main floor. Actually, my mother should have been grateful too. If they'd been down in the basement, she'd have been doing the laundry by herself all the time.

"Are you coming?" my mother asked.

Startled out of my thoughts, I felt embarrassed—too old to be spooked by monsters in the basement. I thundered down the remaining steps, trying to act cool and unconcerned.

My mother knelt down on a small piece of carpet in front of a large wooden box—the cedar chest that had belonged to her mother. It was filled with papers and pictures and postcards and notebooks. She pulled out a large manila envelope.

"I was going through my stuff, and some other things that were down here, to find things that related to your father . . . and to me when I was sixteen." She opened the envelope and pulled out a photograph. "This might be the best place to start," she said.

It was a picture of my father, of course. I wasn't sure but I thought I remembered it. He was smiling—a friendly, confident smile—with his arms folded across his chest. I looked closely at his eyes. Were they my eyes?

"I'm afraid the picture isn't in very good shape," my mother said.

She had that right. The edges were frayed, the tip of one corner gone completely, the colours were faded, and it was stained.

"It's pretty rough," I agreed.

"Well, that's what happens to a photo when it's dragged around every day and then almost flushed down a toilet."

"Flushed down a toilet? Who would do that?"

She pointed at me.

"Why would I try to flush a picture down the toilet?"

"Let me explain. For about three months before you turned four you carried that picture with you everywhere. Sometimes that was a problem. You'd put it down and then forget where you'd left it, and you'd cry and cry and cry until I found it." She laughed at the memory. My mother had such a nice laugh that it always made me smile. "Do you remember any of this?"

I shrugged. Something about it twigged some memories, but not really.

"For a while I thought you were going to grow up left-handed."

"I'm right-handed," I said, raising my right hand.

"I know that. It's just that you always held that picture in your right hand and used your left to pick up a fork to eat or hold a crayon to colour. I think it was your way of having your father around."

"When did I stop carrying it?"

"The day you turned four. The day of your birthday party."

"I must have gotten a lot of presents that day if I finally put the picture down."

"You did get some nice things—at least, I guess you did—but that wasn't it."

"Then what was it?"

My mother didn't answer. She was looking down at her hands, folding and unfolding, kneading her fingers together.

"Mom?"

She looked up. "You have to understand that I was young."

I knew that. What I didn't know was what she was afraid to tell me. My stomach started to tighten.

"You were upset because your father didn't come to your party."

"Was he supposed to come? . . . Wait . . . he died when I was three . . . right?"

She nodded. "And I know I needed to tell you . . . it was just . . . I didn't know how to tell you, or when to tell you."

"You didn't tell me on my birthday, did you?"

"It was just that you were going on and on about him not being there and how he didn't even send you a present."

"Did he ever send me a present?"

"He used to send you presents all the time," she said.

"I didn't know that."

"Maybe I wasn't thinking straight, or maybe I was drinking," she went on.

"Maybe?" I asked, harshly, and then instantly regretted it.

"Okay, I was probably drinking. So right after your party ended I told you that your father was gone. I tried to explain how he couldn't come to your party because he was up in Heaven. I tried to be gentle . . . honestly."

I had no doubts about that. Even as a drunk, my mother had never been mean. Not even when people were mean to her.

"It must have been hard," I said. "I guess I got pretty upset."

"That was the strange part. You didn't get upset at all. At least, you didn't scream or yell or anything. You didn't even cry. You just walked away and went to the bathroom. And when you came back, the picture wasn't with you. I found it in the toilet, still spinning around, but floating on the surface."

"It must have dropped in by accident," I said.

"No. You told me you tried to flush it away. You told me you didn't want the picture anymore because you didn't have a father anymore. I dried it off and decided to put it away somewhere safe until you asked for it again. I thought it would only be a day or so. But you never did ask. A couple of times I tried to give it back to you and you said you didn't want it. That you didn't want any pictures of your father."

"Do you have many pictures of him?"

"Dozens and dozens." She patted the envelope. "Right here. You do want to see them, don't you?"

"Yeah," I answered, although if I'd been completely honest I would have said that I really didn't know.

She pulled out another picture and handed it to me. "This is probably my favourite."

My father looked really young. His hair was a messy mop of brown, his eyes—my eyes— shiny and smiling. "He's wearing his leather jacket," I said.

"He loved that jacket," my mother said. "He would have worn it swimming if he could have. Did I mention that jacket to you before?"

"I guess you did." I didn't want to tell her that it was Candice's father who'd told me about it.

"How old was he when this picture was taken?" I asked.

"I think around twenty-one."

"He looks younger."

"He had to be at least twenty-one because I know this was taken after you were born."

"How do you know that?" I asked.

"Because your diaper bag is in the picture," she said, pointing out the pink, striped bag by his feet. I'd been so intent on looking at him that I hadn't noticed it.

"I always thought he looked so cute when he was carrying that bag. Big, tough guy wearing that leather jacket and carrying a little pink diaper bag." She laughed, and I couldn't help laughing along with her. "Of course, he didn't carry it that often."

No surprise there.

"Because he was usually carrying you."

Now that *was* a surprise.

"You always looked so small in his arms. He loved holding you. You'd often fall asleep snuggled up on his chest while he lay on the couch watching TV."

I tried to picture that. But instead of a picture, I had a feeling in my chest—a warm feeling like I was pressed against somebody.

"Your father always loved babies."

"Shame he didn't like them when they got a little bit older," I blurted out, the words escaping before I was even aware of what I was going to say.

"Your father didn't stop loving you because you got older."

"Then why *did* he stop loving me?" I demanded.

"He didn't."

"Then he had a strange way of showing it, by taking off."

"If he hadn't died he would have—"

"He wasn't there *before* he died!"

"But he would have been . . . I know he would have been . . . it was just a matter of time."

"I guess denial isn't just something people do around alcohol!" I snapped.

My mother didn't answer. She looked shocked. And then hurt. I felt bad. She'd been hurt enough in her life without me adding more on top.

"You knew him better than me," I said. "Maybe he would have come back."

She nodded her head. She had a dreaming sort of look in her eyes. "I know he would have."

"Why did he leave?" I asked.

"Work. He had to travel. That was his job. You can't be part of the circus without travelling."

"My father was in the circus?" I asked. That was a new one for me.

"Not *in* the circus . . . *with* the circus. He was in charge of set-up and making sure all the equipment and all the rides worked and were safe."

"Sounds like he was a handyman."

"He was more than that. Your father and machines . . ." she said, shaking her head. "I guess that sounds like you, as well."

I couldn't figure out how somebody I hardly remembered—who'd been dead before I was even four—could be such a big part of me. I guess, actually, I was a part of him.

"Your father got that job in the circus the strangest way. Let me show you." She poked around inside the envelope and pulled out a newspaper clipping. Was she going to show me a want ad? The paper was old and faded and folded and yellowed. I was afraid it was about to disintegrate.

"I've got to be careful . . . I don't want to rip it any more."

Carefully, delicately, she handed the clipping to me. The headline read "LOCAL MAN IS HERO."

Under that was a picture of a Ferris wheel—and somebody was climbing up one of the spindles, almost at the top of the thing! The figure was little and the face was turned away, but I knew who it had to be.

"We were there at the circus, the three of us, when the Ferris wheel got jammed," my mother said. "And they couldn't get it going again, and there were these two young boys near the top—really not old enough to be on that ride by themselves—and their mother was on the ground, crying and wailing away, and the two boys were up there crying as well. So the boys get all excited and stand up, and one of them looks like he's going to climb right out. People are screaming and yelling at them to sit down and be calm, but you hardly ever get anybody to be calm by yelling at them. So your father hands you to me and he just starts climbing up the Ferris wheel."

"Wow."

"It gave me the heebie-jeebies just watching him— you know how I feel about heights."

My mother wouldn't even go out on the balcony of an apartment—no way she'd even *ride* on a Ferris wheel.

"But your father climbs right up, like he's just going for a stroll, and talks to the kids, and calms them down. Then he climbs back down and *fixes* the Ferris wheel."

"He fixed it?"

She nodded. "He opened up the panel on the side of the machine, borrowed a few tools, and within five minutes he had it working again. The Ferris wheel started turning, the crowd cheered, the mother hugged her kids, and the owner of the circus offered him a job, right there on the spot."

"A happy ending."

"Happy except for the part where he left a week later," she said.

"Oh, yeah. Sorry."

"Don't be. I shouldn't have been surprised. I knew your father wanted to leave. He *hated* the Falls."

I guess that was something else we had in common.

"It was just a matter of where and when." She took the clipping back from me and looked at it. "I wanted us both to go along with him, but he was too wild and too young."

"You were both too young."

"I guess we were. That clipping brought back memories I'd almost forgotten," she said. She looked close to tears. This obviously wasn't any easier for her than it was for me.

"I guess you wish you hadn't saved the clipping."

"I didn't. I didn't even know it was here until I started going through this stuff looking for pictures."

"So Grandma saved it?"

"*One* of your grandmothers."

I gave her a questioning look.

"Do you see those boxes over there in the corner?" she asked, standing up. "Come look."

I followed her across the basement, keeping one eye on the furnace as I walked by.

"These two boxes," she said, touching each with the tip of her foot, "and this crate and this barrel are filled with things that belonged to your father's family."

"My father? Why would his family's stuff be here?"

"Remember I told you that they lived just a few houses down the street?"

"Where the parking lot is now," I said.

"And his mother and my mother were friends. I guess you could say so were your grandfathers . . . at least until I got pregnant."

"That doesn't explain why this stuff is here," I said.

"I'm coming to that. I told you about your father's father and how he had drinking problems. Those problems led to money problems, and they lost their house. They couldn't meet the mortgage payments. So the bank took back the house and they had to leave, but they really didn't have a place to go to— not a permanent place. So when they moved they asked if they could leave some of their things here until they settled in somewhere else."

"And they never came back for it?"

"They ended up moving pretty far away, and then they found out how expensive it was going to be to get the things out there, and one way and another it all stayed here."

"They've been dead for a long time, right?"

"A long time. Your father's mother died about two years after your father died. She took his death pretty hard. I think she died of a broken heart. Nothing's worse than the death of your child . . . especially when it's your only child."

I thought maybe that was aimed at me. "And his old man?"

"He died a year or so after that. I was surprised he lasted that long. Years of alcohol abuse take a pretty hard toll on a body."

"So this stuff," I said, gesturing to it. "Who does it belong to?"

"You, I guess. Your father was an only child and his parents are gone." She shrugged. "I'd forgotten any of this stuff was even down here."

I looked at the containers again, but with a different eye. Whatever was in there belonged to *me*.

"I've just started to scratch the surface," she said. "It's mainly household stuff, like dishes and pots, some books and old records. I suspect it won't be of much value."

"Why not?"

"Valuable things you take with you when you go, or at least arrange to get after you've moved. They didn't do either . . . so . . ."

I guessed that made sense. My fantasies of buried treasure faded.

"But that doesn't mean that there aren't things in there that are really important, though," she said. "I mean, important to you. Things that belonged to your father, to his family, things that might help you to understand your past. I guess you'll find out when you start digging in."

"Me?"

"I think you should be the one to do it. I'll help if you want, but it's your stuff and your history. I'm surprised you aren't more interested."

"I'm interested," I said. "I just don't know if I have the time right now."

"Oh, sorry, I forgot about your very busy schedule," she said, with more than a hint of sarcasm. She paused. "Actually, I've always been surprised that you never asked about your father." She paused again. "Was it because you didn't want to know, or because it hurt too much to ask?"

"Guess it just never came up," I said.

"And now that it has come up, is there anything you want to ask me?" she offered.

I shrugged.

"There has to be something."

"Well . . . I was wondering . . . how did he die?"

"You don't know?"

"If I did know I wouldn't be asking!" I snapped.

"Oh, of course. I know I told you, but it was a long time ago, and you were pretty young, so I guess you don't remember. Your father was hit by a car and killed. The driver didn't stop and they never found him."

"Was he walking or on his motorcycle?" I asked.

"His motorcycle . . . say . . . it sounds like you do remember."

"I guess maybe I remember something," I lied. All I remembered was what Candice's father had said about him racing around on his motorcycle.

"Your father didn't fear speed any more than he feared heights. He used to race around town. The first time I rode on the back of that bike I was so scared, I held on to him so tight that I swear he must have been able to feel my fingernails right through his jacket. Then, when I realized just how good a driver he was, I relaxed a bit."

"Apparently he wasn't good enough," I said, "or he wouldn't have got hit."

"It wasn't his fault. I'm sure of that. Any more questions?"

"Yeah . . . one. Was he a loser?"

She laughed. It was a nervous, surprised laugh. "Why would you ask that?"

"I just want to know," I said.

"Do you think he was a loser?" she asked.

"I didn't know him. Besides, I'm the one asking the questions."

"What do you mean by a loser?"

"You're asking me questions again," I said. "You know what a loser is." I thought maybe she was trying to buy some time, to figure out what she should say. I didn't want her to figure anything out. I just wanted the truth.

"Some people might say he was a loser."

"I don't care about what *some people* think. I want to know what *you* think."

She didn't answer right away. She was gathering her thoughts. "You know, your father never finished high school. He was smart, but he just didn't have any use for some subjects, and he thought a lot of the teachers were just jerks."

"I know that feeling," I said.

"And he had more than his share of fights, and a couple of brushes with the law, although he was never charged with anything. He drank a lot. And of course he got me in trouble, and you were born before I turned seventeen."

"So you're saying he *was* a loser."

"No, I'm telling you why people might think that. But I thought they were wrong."

"Doesn't seem too wrong to me," I said.

"It is. He was a kind man who always treated me well, who was good to his friends, who never hurt anybody, who loved his son."

Loved his son . . . those words hit me in the head and heart and the pit of my stomach all at once.

"So I don't think he was a loser," she said. "He was no angel, but I think if he'd had more time he would have turned it all around. The good would have overcome the bad."

"What about me?" I asked.

"What about you?"

"Am I a loser?"

"You?" She sounded shocked by my question.

I nodded. I didn't even know why I'd asked, because I knew the answer she was going to give. Maybe that was why I'd asked it.

"It's really too early to tell," she said.

"What?" That wasn't the answer I'd expected.

"It's still too soon to tell," she repeated.

"So you think I *could* be a loser?"

"You might."

"But . . . but . . . you don't think my father was a loser," I stammered.

"When he was your age I was positive he was just about the biggest loser I'd ever met. But then I got to know him and saw him start to grow and change."

"And you don't know if I will . . . is that what you're saying? That I'm a loser now who might grow out of it?"

"Of course not . . . well, not exactly. I'm just saying that things could still go either way, and there are lots of things that could make it hard for you."

"Things like what?" I demanded.

"Like not having your father around, like being raised by a drunk."

"You're not a drunk!"

"I was for the first ten years of your life. I still shudder when I think of all the things I did, and the things I didn't do for you."

"You did the best you could," I protested.

"I did the best I knew how, but it could have been a whole lot better. Even without the alcohol, I was still just a kid myself. I don't know any real good seventeen-year-old mothers."

Sometimes it was nice having a mother who was young. She understood things that other people's mothers didn't. Sometimes, though, it was just embarrassing. There were times when I wished she dressed like the other mothers and baked cookies and didn't listen to the same music as me.

"And you know I worry about you and alcohol," she continued.

"There's nothing to worry about."

She gave me a look.

"I don't have a problem!" I snapped.

"I also worry about the people you hang around with," she continued.

"What's wrong with my friends?"

"Can you honestly say that any of them are going somewhere? That they're people who will push you to reach your goals? Is Timmy going someplace in the future other than the unemployment office or the welfare office or jail?"

"Timmy's going to do okay," I said. He'd actually do real okay if he did manage to stay out of jail. "He's a good guy."

"He is that. The kid's got a heart of gold, I'll give him that much. Unfortunately, there's not much going on between those ears. I know you could do more, and he's only going to hold you back. And of course there's his father and his drinking . . . but you don't want to hear what I have to say about that."

"You're right. I don't want to hear. Besides, you think everybody has a drinking problem."

"Not everybody."

"Sometimes it seems like it."

"Sometimes it *feels* like it."

It looked as though we were just headed for another argument. I guess neither of us had any fight left in us. My mother changed the subject.

"So, Jay, are you hungry?"

"I'm always hungry," I said.

"I've got to go out and run some errands. How about if I bring back something to eat?"

"Sounds good."

"Anything in particular you want?"

"Anything from anyplace that has a drive-through window. Surprise me."

"I thought you might have had enough surprises for one day already. Here," she said, as she handed me the envelope. "You hold on to it. These pictures belong to you."

My mother turned and walked away, disappearing up the stairs, leaving me alone, envelope in my hand, heart stuck firmly in my throat.

CHAPTER THIRTEEN

I HEARD THE BACK DOOR CLOSE as I reached the top of the stairs. I was alone in the house. I knew my mother leaving had less to do with her needing to run some errands and more to do with her needing to get away for a while. Maybe it would be better if we just put the whole thing off, put it away again until later, when we'd both be older and better able to handle things. Maybe in a year or so when— There was a loud knocking on the back door. Before I could do anything more than turn around the door popped open and Timmy appeared.

"How's it going?" he asked as he walked in.

"Good. You?"

"It's going good since I found out what I'm having for dinner tonight."

"Dinner?"

"Yeah. It's going to be KFC. You like KFC, don't you?" he asked.

"Who doesn't? But I can't . . . my mother just went out to get—"

"KFC," Timmy said, cutting me off. "I just ran into her and she asked me to join you guys for dinner. She even let me choose the food. That's why it's going to be KFC."

My mother inviting Timmy to dinner—even if she wasn't happy about me hanging out with him— didn't surprise me. She would never have turned anybody away. Or given up on them. It was partly all that AA stuff, but more just who she was. Maybe when you'd been at the bottom yourself, you knew what it's like and were more willing to offer a hand to somebody who was still down there.

"What's in the envelope?" Timmy asked.

I'd forgotten I was even holding it. "Pictures mostly."

"I love pictures, let me see," Timmy said, and he reached out to grab the envelope.

"No!" I snapped and pulled it back. I suddenly felt embarrassed. "I mean . . . they're old pictures, boring pictures. Let's go and watch some TV instead."

I walked over and opened the cupboard above the fridge. I wanted to put the pictures away, and for some reason I wanted them tucked in right beside my mother's secret.

"Hold on a second!" Timmy exclaimed. He reached up and grabbed the bottle of vodka!

"What are you doing?" I tried to grab it back but Timmy pulled it farther away.

"I'm just examining the merchandise. Did you know that was up there?"

"I know it's going *back* up there," I said as I snatched the bottle back from him.

"Hey, no need to get greedy,"Timmy said. "I wasn't going to take all of it."

"You're not going to take *any* of it!" I put it back up in the cupboard, tucked the envelope in beside it, and closed the door.

"Didn't anybody ever tell you that sharing is a good thing? I've always shared with you. Or don't you remember last night? Oh, that's right, you *can't* remember last night," Timmy said, and started chuckling.

"I remember all of last night," I protested. "At least since you explained to me what happened. And I would share that if it were mine to share."

"I know it can't be your mother's, so if it isn't yours, who does it belong to?"

"All you got to know is that it's not yours. Besides, don't you think you drink enough already?"

Timmy chuckled. "Oh, I get it. Are you still hungover?"

"No," I answered. "It isn't that. It's just that . . . maybe we should both slow it down. My mother's an alcoholic, and so is your father."

"My father is not an alcoholic. He's a drunk. A falling-down, stinking, stupid drunk."

"I guess that is different," I said.

"Way different. If you ever want to trade your mother for my father, just let me know."

"Thanks," I said, "but I think I'll hang on to the parent I've got. Doesn't change what I said, though. We both have to think about alcohol."

"I think about alcohol all the time," Timmy said with a laugh.

"I mean about it being a problem. My mother says that stuff runs in families. Don't know if I believe that, though."

"Oh, *I* believe it," Timmy said. "And that's why I drink."

"That makes no sense."

"It makes perfect sense. If it's going to happen anyway, why fight it?"

"What?"

"If I'm going to end up like him anyway, what's the point? I might as well enjoy myself while I can."

"Like I enjoyed myself last night?"

"You *did* enjoy yourself."

"I blacked out!" I exclaimed.

Timmy shrugged. "If I'm going to end up like my old man, then blacking out doesn't seem like the worst thing that could happen."

"Timmy, you are so . . . so . . ."

"Adorable? Smart? Fun at parties?"

"Yeah, right," I snarled.

"Man, you are in one bad mood. Maybe you should go back to bed . . . you did get some sleep this afternoon, didn't you?"

"No."

"Well, that explains it. You're cranky because you didn't get enough beauty sleep. You should have slept it off today."

"I was busy . . . in the basement . . . looking at stuff."

"Stuff?"

"Stuff that belonged to my father's family. There's tons of it, old stuff, nothing but junk."

"Hold on," Timmy said. "Just because something is old doesn't mean it's junk. What sort of things?"

"I haven't looked through much of it. Pots, dishes, old books. Like I said, it's just a bunch of old junk. Nothing valuable."

"You ever watch that show on TV?" Timmy said. "I can't remember the name of it—but people bring in old crap and—"

"I know that show," I said, cutting him off. "It's called the *Antiques Roadshow*."

"Yeah, that's it. And these expert guys look at their junk—ugly, broken stuff that looks like the garbage man would refuse to take it away if it was out on the curb—and some of it's actually—"

"Worth a lot of money," I said, cutting him off again.

"Exactly."

"And you think that something in my basement could be worth a lot of money?"

"How should I know?" Timmy said with a shrug. "I ain't seen it . . . but you never can tell."

I started thinking about it. Wouldn't that be amazing, if I found something in there that was worth a lot of money? Maybe my buried treasure fantasies weren't so stupid after all. And since my mother said that it all belonged to me, then any money I got for selling what I found would belong to me as well. That only made sense. Of course I'd give my mother some of the money to buy something for the house. Our fridge was on its last legs, and who couldn't use a big, flat-screen TV? Most of the money, though, would go to what I wanted—some wheels. I'd been thinking about it for a while. There was no way I could afford a car, but I figured I could buy an old motorcycle and fix it up and I could drive that. I wondered what my mother would think about me riding around on a motorcycle after what had happened to my father. But then again, I was getting a little ahead of myself.

"Come on."

I went down the stairs and Timmy followed close behind. I'd left one light on when I'd rushed upstairs, but the rest of the basement was dark. Each of the light bulbs had to be flicked on individually. I hated walking into the darkness to reach each one. I hesitated for a split second, and Timmy bumped into me.

I knew Timmy didn't mind the basement. He wouldn't even think about things like monsters in the furnace or murderers hiding among the boxes. Timmy hardly noticed the *real* dangers in the world, so I knew he didn't have the imagination to *think up* things to worry about.

"Wow, you weren't kidding when you said there was tons of stuff," Timmy said.

"Isn't your basement the same way?"

"Nope. We don't store anything. If it's broke we throw it out. If it's not broke my old man trades it in at the pawnshop. They must be great places to buy things, because they never give us much for anything we bring there."

Both of the boxes my mother had looked in were still open, and some of the newspapers that had been used for packing were lying on the floor.

"Let's start with these boxes," I said.

"And remember, one man's junk is another man's treasure," Timmy said. "Can't you just see us on that TV show, and we show that dude with the funny accent some piece of garbage and he's so excited he practically takes a crap in his pants, and his voice gets higher and higher and he tells us what we've got." Timmy pulled out a cup and held it up. "And he says something like, *This here cup was actually made by Leonardo da Vinci and—*"

"Timmy, the cup says 'Visit Niagara Falls' on the side, so I don't think it was made by da Vinci."

"Who's telling this story anyway?" he demanded.

Maybe he did have more imagination than I'd given him credit for.

"And it turns out this cup was made by *Ponce de Leons*—does that make you happy?—when he discovered Niagara Falls."

"Ponce de Leon discovered the Fountain of Youth in Florida, not Niagara Falls," I corrected.

"Anyway," Timmy continued, "he says to us . . . he says . . . *So, boys, you are now millionaires!* And he hands us a cheque for a million dollars . . . no, better yet, he actually hands us a million dollars, all in small bills!"

"Like he'd be carrying around a million bucks," I said.

"Why not? He's got a TV show, so he must be rich. Say, what happens if we do find something that's worth a fortune? Do we split it?"

"If we find anything worth a million dollars, I promise you that you'll get a cut."

"Deal," Timmy said as he reached out his hand, and we shook.

BEFORE LONG, THE FLOOR all around us was covered with the things we'd pulled out of the boxes and chests. But it was a safe bet that neither of us was going to be getting rich. What we'd uncovered was lots of stuff that might just as well have stayed buried: pots and pans and mugs—dozens and dozens of souvenir mugs—and books and old records, most of them broken or so warped there was no way they could play, even if we had a record player . . . did anybody have a record player anymore?

After a while Timmy had sort of lost interest. He sat on a beat-up chair he'd pulled over from the corner while he flipped through the pages of one of the old books we'd pulled out. That was one of the few times I'd ever seen Timmy with a book.

I'd thought this was going to be difficult for me. Emotional. It was neither. The only difficult part was all the dust that floated into the air and up my nose. I was sneezing up a storm. I'd thought that because this stuff belonged to my father and his family, going through it would get me thinking, or make me feel sad or happy, or something. Instead, it was just like being at a flea market or somebody's garage sale.

"Wow," Timmy said.

I stopped and looked up. "Wow, what?"

"This guy I'm reading about was amazing."

"I'm just amazed you're reading," I said.

"Me too, but it's not a regular book. It's a scrapbook and it's mostly pictures . . . black-and-white pictures. This guy was a riverman—that's what they called him, because he knew the river so well. It says here that he pulled over one hundred and thirty bodies out of the Niagara River."

"Bodies?"

"Yeah, people who went over by accident, fell or slipped down the banks, and the guys that jumped in to off themselves."

"I don't think many people fall in by accident anymore," I said. "And they like to keep the suicides a secret, but I hear they happen all the time."

"Yeah, all the time. He also saved a bunch of people. At least fifteen people got their lives saved by him, although it might have been better to have let them drown," Timmy said.

"How do you figure that?"

"It says here that he got ten bucks for every body he recovered, but nothing for the people he saved. The guy could have waited awhile and got himself another hundred and fifty dollars."

"Only you would think of that," I said.

"Maybe. Anyway, so this guy lived right here in the Falls, his name is Jamison, and—"

I startled. "What did you say?"

"He lived in Niagara Falls."

"No, his name. What was his name?"

"Jamison."

"William Jamison?"

"No. It says . . . says . . . Harold Jamison."

"Are you sure?" I asked. I rushed over.

"Course I'm sure. It says right—"

I grabbed the book and pulled it away from him. There was a newspaper article, and at the top was a picture, black and white and yellowed and faded and stained, of a man pulling somebody out of the river and through the rocks. Underneath the picture it said *"Harold Jamison pulling another one out of the river."* I looked at the date. The paper was over seventy years old.

"Do you know what my father's last name is?" I asked Timmy.

"I'm gonna take a wild guess and say Jamison, but there's no way this guy is your father."

"Not my father. William is my father. This Harold guy could be my grandfather, or my great-grandfather."

"Or just somebody with the same name," Timmy said.

"And somebody just decided to cut out newspaper articles about somebody who isn't related?" I demanded.

"Maybe he's a cousin. Who knows?" Timmy shrugged.

At that instant I heard the door open and my mother called out a greeting. Maybe there *was* somebody who knew.

CHAPTER FOURTEEN

I RAN UP THE STAIRS and into the kitchen with Timmy right on my heels.

"You two must be *really* hungry," my mother said.

"I'm always hungry, and that chicken smells really—"

"I have to ask you something," I said, cutting Timmy off. "I need you to look at something I found."

"Actually, *I* found it," Timmy pointed out.

"Whatever. Here, look at this."

She put some bags and the bucket of chicken down on the counter and I handed her the scrapbook.

"Did this come from the basement?" she asked.

I nodded. "Timmy was helping me go through things." I pointed down at the open page. "Is this guy related to me?"

She looked at the picture, then scanned the text. "Harold Jamison. Yeah, he is."

"Is he my grandfather?" I asked, trying to put this together with what I knew about him.

"Not your grandfather. Your *father's* grandfather. Your *great*-grandfather."

"Are you sure?"

"Judging by the age of the paper," she said, pointing to the date at the top of the page, "and what I remember hearing about him. My father used to tell me stories about rescues on the river. Your great-grandfather was one of the most famous rivermen of all time."

"And you knew all about this and didn't tell me?"

"You didn't want to know anything about your father, so why would I tell you all about your great-grandfather?"

That made sense . . . but she should have told me anyway.

"The river has always been a dangerous place," my mother said. "It's safer now than in the olden days, since they've put up walls and fences, but people used to slip in accidentally all the time. Your great-grandfather would get them out."

"Dead or alive," Timmy said, ghoulishly.

"He saved the ones he could and retrieved the bodies of the ones he couldn't. Either way, it was dangerous work. But he didn't fear the water, the rapids, the gorge, or the Falls," my mother said.

"Sounds like you," Timmy said, pointing at me. "Not that you've saved anybody, but the not being afraid part."

"I think that runs in his father's family. Jay's father was like that as well," my mother added.

I always felt uneasy when my mother started to talk about my father—especially when she was comparing him to me.

"Can you remember any of those stories you were told?" I asked my mother.

"Some of them. I guess the one that sticks in my mind the most is about your great-grandfather going over the Falls."

"What?" I couldn't believe my ears.

"He went over the Falls—on purpose—and lived to tell about it."

"Man, are you kidding?" Timmy asked.

"No. If this scrapbook is all about him, I'm sure that there has to be some mention of that in here somewhere." She turned toward the back of the book, scanning quickly through the pages, and Timmy and I looked over her shoulders. Page by page, more yellowed clippings from different newspapers.

My mother paused at one page. There was a picture of him—my great-grandfather—holding this girl who was all wrapped up in a blanket. Her hair was plastered back and she looked scared—terrified. He looked big and strong. The story was about how she'd wandered away from her parents and slipped down the bank and into the lower rapids. Harold Jamison had gone down the bank and into the water to get her, saving her life. The story had quotes from her parents and people who had witnessed her fall and rescue. They described my great-grandfather as "brave" and "heroic" and "fearless."

She turned the page. There was another story. This one was about the recovery of a body. Not as exciting, but just as dangerous. It described my great-grandfather going right up to the bottom of the Falls and pulling out a body that had been swirling around there, unable to break free. Apparently, it was a woman whose husband had left her, and she'd thrown herself into the Falls.

Page after page was filled with stories. More interviews, eyewitness accounts, people who were rescued, the families of those who had survived, or not survived, and lots of pictures. Harold Jamison always looked brave and confident, and the people surrounding him looked up to him with admiration.

"He was quite the hero," my mother said. "I remember thinking that it must have been hard for his son—your grandfather—to live up to that."

I didn't know what would be so hard. It would have been nice to have a father that everybody looked up to. Heck, it would have been nice just to *have* a father.

"Here it is," my mother said at last.

Two facing pages had a gigantic headline running across the top: "NIAGARA MAN CONQUERS FALLS." Below the words there was a picture of him—my great-grandfather—and the rest of the space was filled with a story. I started reading.

The article said that Harold Jamison went into the water about half a mile above the Horseshoe Falls, and his barrel was swept over and bounced around in the rapids below for about ten minutes. He was pulled in by the tourist boat, the *Maid of the Mist*. It said he had a bump on his head, some bruises, and sore ribs. The rescuers wanted to take him to the hospital but he demanded to be taken to a pub, where he bought everybody a round of drinks. That *did* sound like my father's family.

"Let me see that," Timmy said as he pulled the scrapbook out of my mother's hands. He started walking away with the book.

"What are you doing?" I called out.

Timmy didn't answer. He crossed the floor and headed down the basement steps.

"Timmy, what are you doing?" I demanded again.

Again he didn't answer. My mother and I both jumped to our feet and rushed after him. My mother looked as confused as I felt. What had gotten into Timmy?

When we got downstairs, Timmy was standing at the far end of the basement, in the midst of all the junk.

"What's going on?" I demanded.

"I'm checking something out," he said.

"Checking out *what?*" my mother asked.

Timmy pointed to the picture in the scrapbook. It was my great-grandfather being pulled out of the barrel.

"Does that look familiar?" Timmy asked.

"Of course it looks familiar. I was just looking at it before you took off with the book and ran down here."

"There was a reason I came down here. The barrel."

"What about the barrel?" I asked.

Timmy looked up and—there it was. The barrel, the same barrel from the old picture, was standing on its end, staring back at us.

CHAPTER FIFTEEN

I LOOKED FROM THE BARREL to the picture and back to the barrel again.

"Oh my goodness," my mother said, her voice barely above a whisper. "Timmy . . . you're right."

"I am . . . and those are words I don't usually hear in the same sentence."

"We have a very, very important piece of Niagara Falls history right here," my mother said.

"It's more than that," Timmy said.

"You're right again. It's also an important piece of *Jay's* history."

"It's still more," Timmy said.

We both looked at him.

"This isn't just important. It's *valuable*."

"Of course it's valuable to us," my mother said.

"No, no, you don't understand. I mean it's worth a lot of money. Lots and lots of money!" Timmy exclaimed.

"This?" I asked. "It's just an old barrel. It doesn't even have a lid."

"It's an old barrel that went over the Falls. You could sell this for a whole barrelful of money."

"Who would want to buy an old barrel?" I asked.

"Lots of people! The Daredevil Museum would, for sure! They've got a whole bunch of barrels and balls and boats that have gone over the Falls."

"That's right," I said. It had been so long since I'd been there that I hadn't even thought about it. Actually, nobody who lived in the Falls ever went to any of the tourist traps.

The Daredevil Museum was one of the dozens and dozens of attractions that lined the strip. Some of them—like horror houses and the Elvis Museum— had absolutely nothing to do with the Falls and were just cheap rip-offs designed to separate bored tourists from their money. A least the Daredevil Museum was real local history.

"Did you mean what you said?" Timmy asked me.

"Depends what I said."

"Don't go and try to weasel your way out of it. Did you mean it when you said you'd give me a share if we found something worth a million dollars?"

"Timmy, there's no way this barrel is worth—"

"But if it is, will you give me a share?"

"Yeah . . . that is . . ." I turned to my mother. "It is my stuff to sell, right?"

"It's yours."

I turned back around to face Timmy. "Whatever it's worth—if it's worth anything—I'll give you some of the money."

"I knew you'd come through," Timmy said as he reached out and shook my hand. "I didn't think you were one of those guys who'd get rich and forget his friends."

"Nobody's getting rich. How do we even know this is the same barrel?" I asked.

"Just look." Timmy took the scrapbook and held it open so the picture was right beside the barrel. It certainly did look the same—but didn't all barrels look just about the same? Besides, even if it was the same barrel, how could we convince anybody it was the real thing?

"Look at these marks," Timmy said, pointing at the barrel.

I looked closer. They were faded letters that looked like they'd been branded into the wood.

"Those are the same as in the picture." He tapped the photo. The markings did look the same.

"So what do we do now?" I asked.

"We go to the Daredevil Museum and talk to the owner about the barrel," he said.

"Do we bring it with us?"

"No," Timmy said, shaking his head. "The barrel stays safe and sound here in the basement. We're only going to move it once we know we have a deal."

"That's good, because I don't think it'll fit into my car," my mother said.

"Probably not. We can always borrow Davie's big brother's pick-up truck if we need to," Timmy suggested. "We'll bring the scrapbook over and show the museum guy the pictures, and if he wants to see the real thing he can come over here."

"You're really thinking this through," my mother said. "I'm very impressed."

"Me too. Impressed and surprised," I added.

"Hey, just because I *choose* not to use my brain most of the time doesn't mean I don't have one. So let's go."

"Not so fast," my mother said, putting a hand on Timmy's shoulder. "First we eat, and then you go."

"Now *that's* good thinking," Timmy said.

"And while we're eating, I want to talk to you boys about something. A favour."

"What sort of favour?" I asked suspiciously.

"It's nothing bad."

"So far it's just nothing."

"And I don't want either of you to get mad."

"At this point I'm just annoyed. So spit it out. What do you want us to do?"

"Okay. It's easy. I think you two should go to a meeting."

"What sort of meeting?"

"Remember when we were talking to my sponsor after that AA meeting? She told me that she talked to you a bit about those meetings where teenagers get together to talk about alcohol and how it's—"

"I don't have an alcohol problem!" I exclaimed. "I come home wasted *one night* and it's like nonstop talking about me having a drinking problem!"

"It's not about *you* drinking. It's about the problems caused for teenagers by other people's use of alcohol."

"That isn't me either!" I snapped. "We don't need to go to those meetings!"

"Speak for yourself," Timmy said.

"What?" I spun around to face him in shocked disbelief.

"I said, speak for yourself. I get screwed over all the time because of my father being a drunk. Tell me more about these meetings."

"The group is called Alateen and it's for teenagers."

"Girls as well as guys, right?" Timmy asked.

"Both, because it affects both. You meet once a week and you get the chance to sit around, have a soft drink and some treats, and talk about problems alcohol has caused for you, and how to cope with them and get on with life."

"Man, I could meet just about every day to talk about that," Timmy said.

"They meet on Mondays—from seven to nine. You could go to the next meeting."

"We could go if we *wanted* to," I said.

"I want to go," Timmy said.

What exactly had gotten into him?

"And Jay wants to come with me," Timmy said. "Right?"

"Yeah, *right*."

"See, he agrees."

"I wasn't agreeing. I was being sarcastic."

"Even if I understood what that meant, you're still coming with me." Timmy smiled. "Right?"

There was no point in arguing . . . at least not right now. A lot could happen between now and then. For example, Timmy could come across a couple of bottles of beer and that would be the end of the idea. Maybe I could try and locate those bottles myself.

"I'll go wherever you go," I said.

"That's wonderful!" my mother said. "Now you two go and get washed up while I put out the chicken."

Timmy followed me up to the main floor and then upstairs to the bathroom. I closed the door behind him.

"You gonna explain this to me?" I asked.

He turned on the tap and picked up a bar of soap. "It's really easy. You get your hands wet and then grab the soap and—"

"The meetings."

"Equally easy. Monday nights, seven to nine. A bunch of people sitting around talking about—"

"I understand all of that! What I don't understand is why you agreed to us going to it."

"Think about it. Soft drinks, some treats, and I'm willing to bet that more than half the people in the group will be girls. We could meet somebody."

I laughed. "So the meeting is just a place where you can eat and maybe get lucky?"

"You have to admit, those aren't bad reasons to go anywhere," Timmy said. "Course there's the other reason, too."

"What other reason?"

"Come on, man. Do you honestly think that neither of us has ever had any problems caused by alcohol?"

I knew the answer to his question. I just didn't want to give it to him. I grabbed the towel and dried my hands before I pushed past him out the bathroom door.

CHAPTER SIXTEEN

THE SIDEWALK WAS CROWDED with sightseers, all walking and gawking and trying to decide which of the dozens of cheesy attractions they were going to go into. The restaurant with the volcano on the roof and the Ripley's Museum seemed to be getting the most business. Timmy and I wove between the throngs of tourists. The lights were just starting to come on—neon lights that kept night from ever being truly dark.

"So, what would you do with a million dollars?" Timmy asked me.

"Buy a better class of friend, for starters."

"You couldn't buy a better class of friend than me. Seriously, what would you do?"

"First off, there's no way this is worth a million dollars."

"Just shut up and let's pretend it is. Until we get there and find out what he really will offer, I want to keep believing it's worth a million. Is that so bad?"

"I guess not."

"So, what would you spend your money on?"

"If it's worth a million, you get two hundred thousand," I said.

"You're kidding me, right?"

"Nope, I told you that you'd get a share. Two hundred thousand doesn't sound too shabby, does it?" I asked.

"Man, you are such a good friend."

I smiled. It wasn't that hard to give away money you didn't have and weren't going to get. I would have offered him an extra fifty thousand if I'd known it was going to make him so happy.

"And what would you do with the rest?" Timmy asked.

"I'd give my mother the same amount I'd give you."

"That still leaves more than a half a million bucks. So?"

"I'd buy a really, really nice car, and I'd have money to go to university and—"

"University? If you had that much money you wouldn't *need* to go to university."

"But I'd want to. And then I'd buy myself a really nice house. Someplace for me and my mom to live."

"You could buy a mansion with that kind of money. Would you buy right by the Falls or more uptown?" Timmy asked.

I laughed. "I'd be uptown . . . in *another* town. If

I had that much money, do you think I'd stay here?"

"Why not? I like the Falls."

"What are you talking about? You're always telling me how boring it is here."

"It wouldn't be boring if I had two hundred grand," Timmy said. "I'd stay right here. This is my home. This is where I belong."

It wasn't where I belonged. If I had that much money I'd move someplace else, and fast. Someplace where there weren't traffic jams or crowds of tourists or neon signs. I wondered if there was anyplace where it was illegal to have neon signs.

"Here we are," Timmy said as we came to a stop in front of the Daredevil Museum. There was nobody waiting in line to get in, and some of the bulbs in the sign were burned out. "Let me do the talking."

"Why should this be any different than usual?" I asked.

We walked up to the ticket booth. There was a little old man, sitting on a stool behind the glass. He looked to be asleep. Timmy knocked on the glass and he startled.

"Sorry to wake you up," Timmy said.

"Wasn't sleeping ... just resting my eyes. You want two tickets?" the man asked.

"We don't want any tickets. We want to talk to the owner."

"Talk to him about what?" the man asked.

"We want to talk to him about this barrel," Timmy said, holding up the scrapbook, open to the page.

The old man stood up and squinted at the picture through the window. "Put it a little closer," he said, and Timmy obliged. The man practically pressed his face against the glass.

"No point in wasting anybody's time," the old man said. "We got lots of artifacts in here, but we don't have that barrel."

"I know," Timmy said. "That's because *we* have it."

The old man scoffed. "Sure you do. And I got the *Mona Lisa* . . . I keep it in my attic."

"I don't know what's in your attic," Timmy said, "but I do know what's in his basement. I also know how pissed off the owner is going to be when he finds out he had a chance to get his hands on this barrel and you turned us down, and it gets bought and displayed over at the Guinness or the Ripley Museum." Timmy turned to walk away.

"Wait!" the old man yelled.

Timmy stopped on the spot. He was facing away from the old man and toward me, so only I could see the smile on his face. He turned around.

"Go inside," the old man said, and he waved us toward the entrance.

"You just have to know how to talk to these people," Timmy said to me.

We pushed in through the doors and found ourselves in a store. There were shelves filled with the usual assortment of Niagara Falls paraphernalia. Mugs and plates and decorative spoons and glass balls filled with scenes from the Falls that snowed when you shook them, and dozens and dozens of other things . . . all ugly, all stuff that nobody could possibly use but everybody seemed to want anyway. There were four people browsing the merchandise and a girl standing behind the counter at the cash register, waiting for them to purchase something.

The old man from the ticket booth tottered into the room. "Where'd you boys find that newspaper article?" he asked.

"Same place we found the barrel . . . in his basement," Timmy said, pointing at me.

"Let me have a look," the old man said.

"We'll show it to the owner," Timmy said, and he clutched the book tightly against his chest.

"That's who I am."

"You're the owner?" Timmy asked. "I thought you were just the ticket-taker."

"In an operation like this, the owner does practically everything. Now, let me have a closer look at that book."

Timmy handed it to him.

"I gotta go and get my reading glasses," he said, and walked off.

"Should we be letting him walk away with the book?" I hissed at Timmy.

"Even if he runs away, how far do you think he could get? Come on, let's look at the displays."

We wandered out of the store and into the back. There were pictures on the walls—black-and-white shots of men and their barrels and the Falls in the background. Underneath each picture was a write-up of what happened. It was a history of all the Niagara daredevils—those who rode the rapids, balanced on tightropes, or tumbled over the Falls.

Then came the first barrel. It was wooden and looked just like the one in my basement. I read the plaque on the wall. It described the first person who went over the Falls and lived—Annie Taylor, a woman! It said she was a retired schoolteacher, sixty-three years old, and she had decided that the way to riches and fame was to stuff a mattress and a pillow into a barrel and go over the Falls. She even took her kitten with her.

"This isn't the real barrel," Timmy said. "It says right here . . . it's a reproduction."

"But that one looks real," I said, pointing to another barrel . . . a massive aluminum one that was painted red and white with a Canadian flag on one end.

"That one *is* real," the old man said as he came back into the room. "Belonged to Rick Munday. He went over the Falls in 1985. At least, that's what he used the *first* time he went over."

"He went over more than once?"

"He tried four times. He got caught twice and made it over twice."

"Twice . . . unbelievable," I mumbled.

"But true. I should know. I'm the guy who pulled him out both times."

"You?" Timmy asked.

"Yeah, me. I wasn't born old, you know, young fella."

"I didn't mean anything," Timmy said.

"That's okay. Tell me about this scrapbook."

"It's from my basement," I said. "It belonged to my grandparents."

"What's your name, son?"

"Jayson, Jayson Hunter. But my father's name was Jamison."

"Jamison? You're a Jamison?"

"I'm a *Hunter*, but my father was William Jamison, and his grandfather was—"

"Harold Jamison," he said, cutting me off.

"You know him?"

"Anybody who knows anything about Niagara knows about your great-grandfather. He was probably the second-best riverman of all time."

"Second-best? Who was the first?" Timmy asked.

"You're looking at him," the man said.

"You?" I exclaimed. "Sorry, I just . . ."

"It says in one of those articles that his great-grandfather pulled out a whole lot of people from the river. I don't remember the numbers, but it's in that book . . . somewhere."

"I know the numbers," the old man said. "At the time of his death, your great-grandfather had saved fifteen people from the rapids and recovered close to a hundred and thirty bodies. My totals are seventeen people saved and *over* a hundred and thirty bodies recovered."

"What's your name?" Timmy asked.

"Fred Williams, but they call me Boomer."

"Boomer Williams . . . I've heard of you," Timmy said. "But I thought you were dead."

"Do I look dead?" he asked.

"Of course not," I said, jumping in before Timmy could answer. "I know you know about my great-grandfather, but did you actually know him?"

"I'm old, but I'm not that old. I knew his son, your grandfather. Course I never did like him very much. He was a drunk and a loudmouth and a bully." He stopped. "Maybe I shouldn't be saying any of this to you. It's not nice to speak bad of the dead, especially to their kin."

"I didn't know him," I said, although all of those things did sound like what I'd already heard.

"And I remember your father," he said. "Big guy. Didn't he rescue some people from some sort of roller coaster or something?"

"A Ferris wheel."

"That's right. I remember reading about it. Thought to myself he was gonna turn out to be like his grandfather. Whatever happened to your dad?" Boomer asked.

"He died in a motorcycle accident."

"Sorry to hear that," he said.

"That's okay. I didn't really know him that well, either. I was pretty young."

"Sorry to hear that, too. A boy should know his father. Lets him know about himself. So, tell me about this barrel."

"It's in my basement—the basement of the house me and my mom live in."

"And you're sure it's this barrel," he said, tapping the book.

"Positive . . . well, almost positive, I guess. Do you want to come and have a look at it?"

"That would be a fine idea. I'll drive you over there. Course I have to wait until the place closes down for the night. Why don't you two look around . . . help yourselves to a T-shirt or something."

"Gee, thanks," Timmy said.

"Yeah, thanks, but you don't have to do that."

Timmy shot me a dirty look.

"It's the least I can do," he said, and Timmy made a beeline for a rack of T-shirts. "Especially with you donating the barrel to the museum."

Timmy spun around on his heels. "Hold on here. Nobody said anything about *donating* nothing."

"What did you have in mind?" Boomer asked.

"The opposite of donate, as in sell, like you get the barrel and we get money."

Boomer turned to me. "I know who *you* are, but who is this guy, anyway?"

"I'm the manager. My name is Timmy . . . Timothy, and I handle all of the business negotiations."

Boomer chuckled. "You're letting *him* make the decisions?"

That did seem like a good question. Was I really letting Timmy make decisions for me? "I guess so," I said reluctantly.

"So what amount are you looking for?" he asked.

"You're the expert. Make us an offer," Timmy said.

"It's hard to put a price on this sort of thing."

"But that price would be a lot," Timmy said.

"Look around." Boomer gestured around the museum. "Does it look like people are beating down the door to see the things I already have?"

There were no more than a half dozen people milling around the museum. He certainly wasn't making a fortune.

"Maybe there would be a crowd if you had our barrel," Timmy said. "Make us an offer."

"I'm not offering anything until I've looked at it. I have to make sure you're not trying to sell me some old pickle barrel."

"It probably is an old pickle barrel," Timmy said, "but one that went over the Falls."

"I guess we'll find out once I see it. First, I've got business to take care of."

"That's cool," Timmy said. "Do you have a bag we can use to put our stuff in?" He was holding a T-shirt.

"No, but the girl behind the counter can give you a bag when she rings in your purchases."

"Purchases? I thought you were *giving* us stuff."

"Giving? Wouldn't that be like making a donation? I was only giving you something when I thought you were giving me something. Business is business." The old man walked away and disappeared behind a door.

"Who'd want one of these T-shirts anyway?" Timmy asked.

"Up until ten seconds ago, *you* did."

"That was because it was for free. I'll take almost anything for free. But that's okay, because the price of the barrel has just gone up by at least the price of two T-shirts."

Timmy looked over at the salesgirl. She sat on a stool behind the counter, filing her nails, working on a big wad of gum, oblivious to us or anybody else in the store.

"Maybe we won't have to wait for this, though," Timmy whispered. He turned away from the salesgirl so his back blocked her view and started to stuff the T-shirt down the front of his jeans.

"What are you doing?" I hissed.

"What do you think I'm doing?"

"You could get us in trouble . . . you could get caught," I whispered.

"I *will* get caught if you don't *shut up*."

I watched out of the corner of my eye, helpless, as the T-shirt disappeared down his pants. I moved away. I couldn't stop him, but at least I could get away from him. Being arrested for shoplifting didn't seem like the best way to start negotiating a business deal.

I picked up a book from the shelf, *The Daredevils of Niagara*. I started flipping through the pages. Right there on the first page was a picture of the first person who went over the Falls, Annie Taylor, that teacher I'd just been reading about on the plaque over the barrel. She looked like a tough old bird. I turned a couple more pages and there, staring back at me, was my great-grandfather. He was standing beside his barrel— the barrel he'd used to go over the Falls—the barrel that was sitting in my basement. Wow . . . my relative.

"You two ready to go?" Boomer asked as he reappeared.

I was startled out of my thoughts. "I thought we had to wait until you closed?"

He turned to the salesgirl. "Crystal, when you finish up with those nails I want you to close up, okay?"

She looked up and gave him a bored nod of agreement.

"Let's go," he said.

"Wait," I said. "I want to buy this book."

"Don't worry, it's yours. You two head out through the front. I'm parked in the back. I'll swing around and get you."

"Sure, meet you out front."

Timmy flashed me a smile as Boomer walked off. "He's desperate," he whispered. "This is gonna be like taking candy from a baby . . . or an old man. Same thing. Neither has any teeth and they both need a diaper."

Timmy laughed at his own joke. I didn't. I was just grateful he'd kept his voice down and Boomer hadn't heard him. Boomer was old, but there was something about him that didn't *seem* old. I could picture him balling his fingers into a fist—a wrinkled fist covered with age spots—and busting Timmy in the nose.

CHAPTER SEVENTEEN

I OPENED THE BACK DOOR and Timmy, followed by Boomer, walked in. My mother was at the sink washing up the dinner dishes.

"Hey, Mom."

"Hello boys. I was on the phone with Sarah Bayliss and she said you were very welcome to come to the next meeting and . . ." She turned around and stopped mid-sentence when she saw Boomer. I could tell by the look on her face that she was wondering who he was and why he was there with us.

"This is Mr. Williams," I said.

She dried her hands on her apron. "I'm pleased to meet you, Mr. Williams," she said as they shook hands.

"My pleasure, ma'am. Let's forget that Mr. Williams stuff, though. You can just call me Boomer. Everybody else does."

"Sure. I'm happy to meet you, Boomer . . . Boomer Williams. *You're* Boomer Williams? *The* Boomer Williams?" Her look of confusion returned.

"That's me. I don't suppose they made a second one."

"I'm *really* happy to meet you. I thought that you were . . . I mean . . ."

"I thought he was dead too," Timmy said, completing her thought.

My mother now looked embarrassed. But Boomer just laughed. "That's okay. Obviously I'm not getting out enough if everybody thinks I've kicked the bucket. The boys came by the museum to talk to me about a barrel."

"They told me that's what they were going to do. Are you here to see it?"

He nodded. "To see if it's authentic . . . if it's okay with you that I look at it."

"Of course! Please, feel free. I'll put on a pot of coffee . . . would you like some coffee?"

"Never said no to a cup and I'm not about to start now."

"Great. You go downstairs and I'll put on the coffee and clean up."

"You don't have to clean up by yourself. I'll help," I offered.

"No, you go downstairs. I'd just as soon stay up here anyway . . . that basement has spooked me since I was a kid. Don't laugh, but there's something about that furnace that unnerves me."

"I promise I won't laugh," I said. But I also wasn't going to tell her that it had the same effect on me—especially not in front of other people. "Come on, let's go and have a look at the barrel."

I led the way down the stairs with Boomer and Timmy trailing behind. I flipped on the main switch and then pulled on the other lights as I got to them.

"There it is," I said.

Boomer walked over and placed his hand against the side of the barrel. He ran his hand up and down the wood and then looked inside. "What's all this stuff?"

"Things that belonged to my grandparents. They used it to store things."

"That's awful! We need to get everything out so I can have a look at it, proper like."

Quickly Timmy and I unloaded the barrel. I reached in, grabbing things and handing them to Timmy, who put them on the floor—dishes, pots and pans, and assorted kitchen stuff, including an old toaster and a waffle-maker. When the barrel was about halfway empty I had to bend over and reach right down inside, so there was about as much of me inside the barrel as out. The first time I did that it felt a little bit eerie. My great-grandfather had put his entire body inside there, had the top put on and sealed, and then gone over the Falls. A shudder went through my body at the same time as a buzz went through my brain.

I tipped the barrel onto its side and started pulling out the remaining items. After taking out the last thing—a big pot—I lifted the barrel back up so it was sitting on its end again. It was a big barrel and it had some weight to it.

"There, it's empty," I said.

Boomer came over and started looking at the barrel while Timmy and I stood off to the side. He walked around it, tapping on it with his fingers, running his hands along its length. He had a picture—the one from the book with my great-grandfather standing beside his barrel—and he kept looking from the picture to the real thing . . . or I guess what I *hoped* was the real thing.

He pulled a tape measure out of his pocket and measured the height and then the circumference of the barrel. He stuck his head inside, and for a second I thought he was going to climb right in. He grabbed the rim and tipped it back onto its side. I knew the barrel was fairly big and heavy but he made it look effortless. He was a strong old bird. Finally he stood up and brushed off his pants.

"I was worried when you told me it was in a basement," Boomer said. "Figured the whole thing would be nothing more than rotten wood."

"It's in pretty good shape, I think," I said.

"Not pretty good. Perfect. This basement is dry, so there's no rot whatsoever."

"And is it . . . is it real?" I asked.

He smiled. "I don't think there's any doubt."

I felt as if a gigantic weight had been lifted off my shoulders—a weight I hadn't fully realized was there until it was gone.

"Okay," Timmy said, "not only is it the real deal, but it's in great shape. So how much money are we talking?"

"I think before we start talking money we should all go upstairs and have Jay's mother be part of the discussion," Boomer said.

"It's Jay's barrel," Timmy said.

"Maybe so, but I still want his mother involved. Don't want anybody to say I cheated a young boy . . . especially a relative of Harold Jamison's."

WE SAT AROUND the kitchen table, drinking a third cup of coffee. It seemed like we were talking about anything and everything *but* the barrel.

"So, you like working at that casino place?" Boomer asked my mother.

"It's not bad. People are friendly, pay is okay . . . good benefits package . . . dental, health, prescription drugs and everything."

"That's important. Especially when you get older."

"And my boss is pretty nice," my mother continued.

"I wish mine was nicer," Boomer said.

"I thought you worked for yourself, that you owned the museum," I said.

"I do own the place and I do work for myself. You boys might find out if you ever own your own business that the worst boss you can ever have is yourself. I gotta work evenings and weekends and holidays, can't phone in sick and take a day off. No overtime pay, bonuses, or paid vacations. And worst of all, I can't fire myself."

"More coffee?" my mother asked.

"I'd love another one," he said as he held his cup out to her, "but I probably shouldn't."

My mother took his cup, stood up, walked over to the counter, and refilled it. "A little coffee never hurt anybody," she said as she handed him back the cup.

"I guess that's the problem. I think this is about my twentieth cup today."

"Twenty!" we all said at once.

"I'm sort of addicted to the stuff."

"There are worse things to be addicted to," my mother said.

I had a terrible feeling that she was going to go off on one of her AA lectures.

"That's for sure, but I don't even touch any of that other stuff. I don't think I've had a drink for forty years."

"Do you belong to AA?" my mother asked, and I cringed.

Boomer snorted. "Not me! Never. I'd never go near one of those meetings!"

I knew I liked this guy.

"A bunch of people sitting around bellyaching about alcohol having power over their lives and such. If drinking is a problem, then just stop drinking!"

"You make it sound easy," my mother said.

"Far as I can see it is easy. You just gotta stop putting the stuff in your mouth and . . ." He quit talking and looked directly at my mother. "Shoot, you're one of those AA people, aren't you?"

"I've been sober and dry for five years."

"Five years and a day," I added.

"I didn't mean no disrespect. Whatever you need to do to stop drinking is a whole lot better than drinking. It really wasn't a problem for me to begin with."

"Then why did you stop?" Timmy asked.

"I just didn't see the point. Stuff doesn't taste very good, costs lots of money, and doesn't do you any favours. So I just stopped. Wasn't hard."

"For some of us it *is* hard. We had to understand and accept that we were powerless over alcohol before we could quit."

"Maybe that's where I have an advantage. Spending my time on the river, I learned what 'powerless' meant real early on. Saw that time and time again." Boomer paused, and in his silence I wondered if he was thinking about those days. "Course, the river can have the opposite effect, too. Can cause people to drink. I think that was what it was like for your grandfather," he said, looking at me.

"I don't understand."

"I don't think it was easy for him," Boomer said.

"Or easy for anybody who had to be around him," my mother said.

"Don't get me wrong. I'm not excusing him— I didn't even like him. Heck, if we're gonna be real honest, I thought he was a jerk. But I still understand some of it. It would have been hard for him, being the son of a man like his father. Your great-grandfather was a hero. He cast a big shadow. All men long to live up to their fathers."

I wouldn't have known anything about that. Invisible men didn't cast a shadow.

"Your grandfather tried, but he couldn't fill his father's shoes. He was no riverman . . . just too scared of it."

"And you weren't afraid?" I snapped. I didn't understand why I was defending my grandfather. I knew hardly anything about him, and the little I did know I didn't like. So why did I feel so angry?

"There were many days when I was scared. Sometimes I was terrified. Only a fool wouldn't be afraid of something that big and strong and powerful and unpredictable."

"Then what's the difference between him and you?" I asked.

"In some ways, not much. It's just that I used the fear to keep me sharp, keep me alive, and keep other people alive, too. I knew when to be afraid."

"And my grandfather didn't?"

Boomer shook his head. "He was afraid all the time he was around the river."

"That's like me," my mother said.

"He tried to hide it by acting brave and blustery, but people could tell. I could tell. And because he was afraid all the time he couldn't rely on his head to be clear, to think, or listen to his gut to let him know he really was in danger. Some people can stand right at the edge of a cliff without getting nervous."

"Now that sounds like you, Jay," Timmy said.

My mother's eyes opened wide. Why? It wasn't like she was hearing something that she didn't already know about me and heights.

"Jay can stand right on the edge of the gorge and not even blink," Timmy continued. "He does it all the time."

I didn't want to even look over at my mother now. The heights part she knew, standing at the edge of the gorge she didn't. Or how often I went there, stood there, just to look all that way down . . .

"I don't really get that close," I said.

"Are you joking?" Timmy exclaimed. "I've seen you practically—"

I shot Timmy a dirty look and he shut up. "I only stand where I know it's safe."

"That's the key," Boomer said. "Knowing where it's safe and where it's not. Knowing what you can and can *not* do. Not letting fear fog your brain. That's what was right with your great-grandfather and lacking in your grandfather. Fear makes for bad decisions. And because of his fear and those bad decisions, he started to drink. Maybe it was to calm his nerves, but it only made it worse." Boomer stopped. "Maybe I shouldn't be talking like this, not to family members."

"He's not my family," I said. "I didn't even know the guy."

"Know him or not, he *was* your family. And you should be proud of your great-grandfather, and proud that you share something with him and—"

"More coffee?" my mother asked, cutting Boomer off.

"Still working on this one."

"Do you boys know that Boomer was involved in the most miraculous rescue in the history of the Falls?" my mother asked.

Timmy and I both shook our heads.

"What happened?" I asked.

"Nothing special," Boomer said. "I pulled a girl from the river, that's all."

"If he won't tell you about it, I will," my mother said. She turned to Boomer. "If I get anything wrong, then you correct me, okay?"

Boomer nodded.

"There was a young girl who was being swept down the river, and Boomer reached out and grabbed her . . . a dozen feet before she was swept over the Falls."

A shiver went up my spine as I tried to picture it.

"I was in the right place at the right time, and she was close enough for me to grab. Just lucky," Boomer explained.

"It was more than luck. There had to be dozens of people standing there," my mother said.

"More like hundreds," Boomer said.

"And of those *hundreds* you were the only one to react."

"That's not true. There was me and a Parks worker. He was holding me when I reached out to grab the girl. If it wasn't for him, me and the girl both would probably have gone over together."

"But why was she in the river to begin with?" Timmy asked.

"A family friend took her and her brother for a boat ride and the engine conked out."

I noticed that Boomer was the one telling the story now—*enjoying* telling the story.

"They got caught in the current, pulled into the rapids, and the boat tipped, throwing them into the drink."

"Unbelievable," I said. "She must be the luckiest person in the world."

"I think that honour belongs to her brother. He went over the Falls . . . and lived."

"What?" I gasped.

"He went over the Falls wearing nothing but a life jacket and lived to tell about it. He was pulled out of the water by the *Maid of the Mist*. Alive, well, unharmed, except for a few bumps, bruises, and cuts."

"That's impossible."

"I would have said so myself. I thought it was a one in a million chance, until that man went over last year and lived."

"I remember that,"Timmy said.

"The good Lord protects fools and small children," Boomer said.

"What about the other guy?" Timmy asked. "The guy driving the boat with the kids."

"He went over the Falls too. I saw him. Close enough to see the look on his face, the look of terror, but not close enough to do anything . . . anything except remember that look forever."

"And he died, right?"Timmy asked.

"They never even found his body."

"Being there on the edge, grabbing that girl, that must have been terrifying," I said.

"It was, but I wasn't really scared at the time. It all happened so fast. It wasn't till later that I got scared. I'm holding the little girl in my arms and she refuses to let me go. She has a grip on me, digging her fingers right into me. And she's crying for her brother and shaking, and then I started shaking too. Then it was me who didn't want to let go of her. I didn't want anybody to know it was me doing the shaking." Boomer looked down at his coffee.

"All fascinating stuff," Timmy said. "But enough about the past, I'm more interested in the future. Like, how much money are you going to be offering us for the barrel?"

"I was thinking a thousand dollars."

"A thousand dollars!" Timmy exclaimed. "You gotta be joking, and I don't think it's that funny a joke. How about *ten* thousand dollars?"

"Now you're the one doing the joking," Boomer said.

"You're right. Ten thousand dollars is a joke. I should have said *twenty-five* thousand!"

Boomer laughed out loud. "Now you're not joking, you're hallucinating! Did you think that old Ford of mine—the one I drove you over in—was a Mercedes in disguise? Twenty-five grand is way, way out of my league."

"Then maybe we should go and talk to somebody who's in that league. Maybe the guy who runs the Ripley's Museum."

"Try all you want. First off, he probably won't pay you near that much, and he definitely won't pay anything unless he knows it's the real thing."

"We know it's the real thing," Timmy said.

"Maybe you know it, but that Ripley's guy won't buy anything until he hears from his expert," Boomer said.

"Fine, let him bring his expert here too,"Timmy said.

"His expert has already been here." Boomer pointed to himself.

"You?"

"That's right. And who knows, maybe I can't guarantee him, one thousand percent, that it's real."

"But you just *said* it was real!"Timmy exclaimed.

"I'm old. I forget things. How about two thousand dollars?"

"For two thousand dollars it can just sit down there in the basement and rot. Hell, for that price I might as well chop it up and use it for firewood."

"You think that's some sort of threat?" Boomer asked.

"No threat,"Timmy said. "I'm just so stupid that I'd rather burn it than be cheated. So make us an offer that makes sense or——"

"You can have it for two thousand dollars," I said to Boomer.

"Jay, shut up! Let me handle things. We can get more than that. I'm sure I can sell it for——"

I turned directly to Boomer. "For two thousand dollars you can have it in your museum . . . for two years. I'll rent it to you."

"Rent it?"Timmy questioned. "That makes no sense!"

"Actually, it makes perfect sense," Boomer said. "You got yourself a deal," he said as he reached across the table to shake hands.

"No! No deal!" Timmy grabbed my hand before we could shake. "We gotta talk . . . privately?"

"No," I said, shaking my hand free from his grip. "Is that a deal?"

"I think it is, but on one condition," Boomer said.

"What sort of condition?" I asked.

"Good help is hard to get—you've seen Crystal. I need some help at the museum. I'd like you two to work for me."

"You want *us*?" I asked.

"Nothing too fancy. Some evenings and weekends. Minimum wage. You could keep an eye on your barrel, as well."

Timmy looked at me and I looked at him. He shrugged.

"You got yourself a deal," I said, and Boomer and I shook hands.

CHAPTER EIGHTEEN

I TOSSED AND I TURNED. I couldn't get to sleep. My mind was going around and around. I was thinking about what I was going to do with two thousand dollars . . . well, really, twelve hundred bucks. I was going to give Timmy four hundred and four hundred to my mother to help pay for a new roof, but the rest was mine. That was more money than I'd ever had in my entire life, more than I thought I'd ever have unless I won a lottery or something. Should I save it for a car, or maybe put it away for school, or just piss it all away? I wondered which decision would be the smart one, and which one would make me look like a loser? I couldn't seem to come up with an answer and I couldn't sleep.

Maybe if I went downstairs and got a glass of milk, maybe watched some TV, I might be able to get tired enough to fall asleep.

I opened my bedroom door and saw that a light was on downstairs. Was my mother still awake, or had she fallen asleep in front of the TV herself? Quietly I went down the stairs, following the light that I now saw was coming from the kitchen. I walked in. My mother was sitting at the kitchen table with her back to me.

"Hello," I said softly, and she shrieked and practically jumped into the air.

"You scared me!" she exclaimed.

"I was trying *not* to scare you!"

My mother was jumpy and startled easily. Sometimes she'd be walking down the street, lost in thought, until she practically bumped into somebody walking toward her. Then she'd scream, and nearly scare the heck out of everybody for blocks. I'd learned to expect it, but sometimes it still took me by surprise.

"What are you doing up?" she asked.

"How about I ask you the same question?"

"Do you want some hot chocolate?"

"That would be nice, maybe with some of those little marshmallows."

"Do we have little marshmallows?" she asked.

I opened the cupboard and pulled out a bag of mini-marshmallows. I also grabbed the container of hot chocolate mix. "You didn't actually know if we had hot chocolate, did you?" I asked.

"Not really."

Since I did most of the grocery shopping I almost always had a better idea what we had and what we didn't have.

My mother filled the kettle and put it on the stove, turning on a burner. I set the hot chocolate and marshmallows down on the counter and she got two big mugs.

"You know, we have to talk about that," she said.

"Talk about what?"

"About you doing the shopping."

"What about me doing the shopping? I do a really good job—"

"I know, you do a *great* job. It's just that I was thinking that . . . maybe it's time for *me* to start doing it again."

"You?"

"Don't sound so surprised. I can do the shopping, you know. I did it for years when you were little. Did you think the groceries were delivered by the Food Fairy?"

"Of course not." What I did remember was that the food often wasn't delivered at all. When I was really little I used to go grocery shopping with her. Then, when I was older, I was the one who'd go out and get a few things at the store—things like milk and bread when we had nothing. Finally, when I was about twelve, I'd just started doing it all myself.

"So no arguments and no questions . . . unless you have a question?"

"No . . . you want to do the shopping, be my guest . . ." I paused.

"Go on," she said, although the look in her eyes made me think that she really didn't want me to. She looked nervous about what I was going to say.

"Well, since we're both up and you're clearly in the mood for questions, I was just wondering . . . why didn't you ever tell me anything about my great-grandfather, about how famous he was, what a hero he was?"

"Like I already told you. I just figured if you didn't want to hear anything about your father, you probably didn't want to hear anything about your great-grandfather."

"Is that the only reason?"

The kettle started whistling and my mother reached over and took it off the burner. She poured boiling water into the two mugs and then shovelled in two heaping spoonfuls of cocoa powder. She set them down at the table.

"Bring over the marshmallows," she said, and sat back down.

I sat down at my usual spot, across the table from her. I took a spoon and stirred until the powder had all dissolved, and then I added marshmallows— fifteen, for fifteen years old.

"So was there any other reason?" I asked again.

She kept stirring her mug, looking down at the swirling brown whirlpool she was creating, like the answer was going to be there. She reminded me of a fortune-teller reading the leaves in a teacup. But the only answer it gave was the *ting* of spoon against ceramic. Then, just when I thought she wasn't going to answer at all, she looked up directly into my eyes.

"I was scared." She *looked* scared now.

"Of what?"

She pointed at me.

"You were scared of me?"

She shook her head. "Not *of* you. *For* you." She reached across the table and gathered up my hands, holding them in hers. "Let me try to explain." She gave my hands a gentle squeeze but didn't let go. "You know how much I love you, how I'd give up my life for you in a second. You know that, right?"

I nodded my head slightly. I knew. I wondered if she knew I felt the same way about her.

"I was afraid of what you could become."

"I'm not going to become an alcoholic!" I snapped, anger surging through me. I tried to get my hands free but she held on with surprising strength.

"Please, listen. That isn't what I was going to say."

I stopped struggling and she continued to hold on.

"It isn't just alcoholism that is passed through the genes. It's so much. I remember the first time I realized you had your father's eyes. And then I noticed you hold your head the way he did, tilted to the left, when you're confused or worried."

I realized my head was tilted that way right now and I straightened up.

"The way you phrase words, some of the foods you like and dislike—that's just like him too, even though I know you didn't learn it from him."

"Yeah, so we like the same foods, so what?"

"And then you started to build things. First with blocks, and then Lego, and then how you loved to use tools to make things. The go-kart, the mini-bike."

"Like my father," I said softly.

"And you liked me to drive the car fast, and you seemed to be fearless around heights. Like your father and your great-grandfather. And that's what worries me. It's important to be afraid of things."

"What?" I demanded.

"Fear is important because it helps keep you alive."

"According to Boomer, fear is what gets you killed. He said fear fogs the brain."

"He said *too much* fear is dangerous. Not being afraid can get you killed just as fast. Like it killed your father and your great-grandfather."

I knew about my father. "How did my great-grandfather die?"

"On the river, trying to rescue somebody."

"At least he died a hero."

"He died trying to be a hero. The man was already dead, and when it was all over your great-grandfather was dead as well. Hero or no hero, he was dead."

"You seem to know a lot about him," I said.

"I do now. I've been reading that book you brought home yesterday." She tapped her finger against the book. I hadn't noticed it sitting there on the table along with the newspaper and some magazines. "You should read this," she said as she slid it across the table to me.

"I have . . . at least, I started to."

"You might want to read it all, but maybe tomorrow would be better." My mother took another big sip from her hot chocolate and stood up. "I'm going to bed now, and you should probably do the same."

"I'm not sleepy. I'm going to watch a little TV."

"Just a little. You have a big day tomorrow. What time do you start working?"

"Boomer said to be there around eleven so he could train us. How about you, what shift are you on tomorrow?"

"Noon to eight, so I'll be here when you get home."

"I'll be here way before that. He's only going to keep us until around five."

"I meant when you get home from your Alateen meeting," she said.

I'd forgotten all about that. Unfortunately, she hadn't.

"You are going, aren't you?"

"Yeah . . . probably . . . unless something comes up."

My mother rinsed out her mug and put it in the sink. She walked back, gave me a hug and a kiss on the top of my head. "Let's hope nothing comes up. I'll see you in the morning."

I CLOSED THE DOOR quietly, so quietly that I could hardly hear it shut. That meant that there was no chance that my mother, two floors up, would have heard anything. I moved down the driveway as silently as possible, but my footsteps still echoed ever so softly off the wall. It was amazing how in the dead of night every sound seemed loud. I hung a left out of the driveway, headed down the street, and walked quickly until I'd put a couple of houses behind me. I took a deep breath—I'd been holding my breath up until then.

The air was cool and moist. No surprise there. When you lived this close to the Falls the air was almost always that way. Even in the middle of the summer, in the middle of a heat wave, it was cool at night. As the sun sank, the mist was carried along on the breeze until it blanketed the whole city.

I looked at my watch. It was just past four in the morning. There was nobody on the street. Again, no surprise. All the people who had been out drinking or gambling or partying had gone home, and the people who had to get up early for work were still sleeping. The street basically belonged to me—me and a stray cat that darted out between two parked cars.

At the first cross street I looked to my left and caught a glimpse of Clifton Hill. The neon lights still glared but there was nobody on the street to see them shine. The sidewalks were deserted and the street was empty. A police car shot across the intersection, appearing and then disappearing in a flash. I guess I wasn't completely alone.

What would a cop do if he saw me out here? Would he stop and talk to me or give me a hard time? It wasn't like I was doing anything wrong. I was just out for a walk, and it wasn't like it was illegal to go for a walk . . . was it? But then again, it was late and I wasn't sixteen. Actually, how the hell would he know how old I was? I could say I was sixteen, maybe even seventeen or eighteen . . . Okay, sixteen. I could probably get away with that. Maybe it would be better not to talk to a cop to begin with. Maybe it would be better to just go home. No, I didn't want to do that.

As I continued down the street the sound of the Falls got louder. The noises of the day were all gone, stripped away, leaving the water to sing by itself. Up ahead, overtop of the houses, I caught my first glimpse of the column of mist rising up into the sky. What would it have been like for the first explorers to see that in the distance? They would never have believed what their eyes were seeing.

A car flashed by on the road in front of me. Then another. I stopped at the edge of the road that ran along the river. There was more traffic than I would have thought, and there were people on the sidewalk, looking down at the gorge. I didn't imagine I'd be completely alone, but I was surprised at the number of people who were still out. Not thousands or even hundreds, but I could see at least a dozen or so. What were they doing there at that time of the night? Maybe the same thing as me. Maybe none of them could sleep either. Everybody was walking in the same direction, toward the Falls. It was like a magnet pulling us closer.

I cut across the grass to reach the walkway. The lawn was slick and wet, and as I passed by some bushes I noticed a guy—a bum—lying there. He could have been just sleeping, but more likely he'd had too much to drink and had passed out. Maybe that was what I needed to help me sleep, a beer or two. Couldn't hurt, right? But that made me think of Timmy's Amaretto, and that nearly made me bring up the KFC.

I came up to the railing and looked down. There was a slight outcrop of rock and then a sheer drop to the rocks and river. There was enough light for me to see the water below—rolling, rushing, boiling past rocks, racing and rushing down the gorge. Hypnotizing. Timmy was right, I could stare at it for hours, until it almost seemed like it was a part of me, calling to me. And it was strange, because I'd seen the river a million times before, but tonight it was like I was seeing it for the first time. It used to be that I could almost imagine I *was* the water, swirling, rushing over the rocks, plunging into the gorge, but now, instead, I was picturing a man among the rocks, in the rapids, rescuing people, or retrieving those that couldn't be rescued. I was picturing my great-grandfather. Brave. A hero. A daredevil who went over the Falls in a barrel—the barrel that sat in my basement.

I'd finished reading about him—how he did it—how he went over the Falls. He went in from the Canadian side, about five hundred metres upriver from the Falls itself. To test the currents he put in another barrel first. It was identical to the one he was going to use, and it was packed with a bag of sand that weighed the same as him. He needed to see where the current was going to take it. That was important. At some places along the base of the Falls there were rocks piled up, rocks that would smash anything that went over the edge. Hitting them would be instant death. He sat there watching his test barrel go over just the way he wanted and hoped his barrel would do the same. I think I would have waited until I'd heard what happened to that barrel. Sure, it went over the Falls, but did it survive? Did it get caught up in the undertow or did it pop free? But he didn't wait. They sealed him in the barrel, gave it a push, and he was gone.

As I approached the Falls there actually was a little crowd. The spot along the fence closest to the brink was ringed with people. They were drawn to this spot. Moths to a flame.

I had to wonder about these people. They didn't look like the regular cross-section of tourists. There were no kids, only a couple of women, and no Japanese folks clicking away with their cameras. In fact, I didn't notice anybody taking any pictures. They all just stood there, staring out at the water. Rather than taking pictures with cameras, I thought, they were storing the images in their brains, experiencing it first-hand, without a lens in between to make the experience less real.

How many of these people had been drinking? How many had been at the casino until closing, trying desperately to win back the money they'd lost, and only losing more? And now they didn't want to go home. That meant facing the wife and trying to explain how the mortgage wasn't going to be paid because they didn't have the money. And there wasn't any answer or way out except to . . . a chill went up my spine that had nothing to do with the cool mist that surrounded me. Was there somebody here who was thinking about ending it all, about jumping over the railing?

I looked from face to face, trying to read the sideways glimpses of their expressions. How could I possibly know what they were thinking, how they were feeling, even if a part of me understood the temptation? And even if I could have seen inside their heads, what would I have done if somebody suddenly

put a foot up on the railing and heaved himself up and over and leaped forward? They'd be gone in a split second, and no power on earth would be able to save them.

I turned slightly and was startled to notice two cops standing just off to the side. They were watching the people watching the Falls. I wondered if they were trying to figure out what I'd just been thinking about. Suicides were bad for business, bad for the casinos. Although I could imagine an advertising campaign aimed at a whole new market: the people who wanted to off themselves, and the ones who wanted to watch. People loved to watch.

I'd read that in the olden days, thousands and thousands of people would gather along the river if there was even a hint that something was going to happen. Smart business people used to give false hints all the time, but there were lots of real stunts, too. Shooting the rapids, going over the Falls, tightrope walks across the gorge. Daredevils were good for business. Now it was just illegal. Anybody trying to pull a stunt would be arrested and given a huge fine, maybe even sent to jail . . . or a psychiatric hospital.

"Hello, son."

I startled out of my thoughts. The two cops were standing right in front of me now. They looked familiar. I'd probably seen them around.

"Are you okay?" the larger of the two asked.

"Sure . . . of course," I stammered. "Why are you asking?"

"You just looked a little lost," he answered.

"And a little young," the shorter of the two asked. He was actually very short. I was taller than him by at least a couple of inches.

"How old are you?" the second one asked.

"Seventeen. Well, almost seventeen."

"I see," he said, with a tone that meant he didn't believe me. "Do you have any I.D. on you?"

"No, nothing," I said, patting my empty pockets. I didn't have my wallet. I didn't even have a quarter with me.

"Are you with somebody?" the larger officer asked, gesturing to the crowd ringing the river.

"No, I'm by myself."

"How did you get here?"

"I walked. I live here," I said, pointing in the general direction of my house. "On Pine Street. One Seventy Pine."

"A local boy. You look a little familiar but I don't think we've had any dealings with you."

"That's a good sign," the smaller one added. "So why are you out here alone in the middle of the night instead of home on Pine Street sleeping in your bed?"

"I couldn't sleep so I thought I'd go for a walk."

"To the Falls?"

I shrugged. "Where else is there to go in the middle of the night?"

"You have a fight with your girlfriend?" the big cop asked.

"I don't have a girlfriend right now."

"How about you and your old man. Did you get kicked out of the house? Is that why you're here?"

"'Cause if that's the case we can bring you someplace for the night," the other guy added.

"I live with my mother, and she didn't kick me out. I just wanted to go for a walk. Is that against the law?" I snapped, getting annoyed at their questions.

"No, it's not against the law, but it isn't smart to start giving us attitude. Understand?" The big cop's tone of voice was suddenly hard.

"We're just trying to do our job, kid. We just want to make sure you're okay out here."

"Of course I'm okay and . . ." I suddenly realized why they were asking me these questions. They were afraid that I was going to . . . "I'm not going to jump," I said.

"What did you say?" the smaller one asked.

"I'm not going to jump."

"Could you please step away from the railing," the little cop said.

"What?" I didn't really understand what he meant. I didn't move.

"Step away from the railing. Now!" the bigger cop ordered.

I stumbled toward the two officers.

"Please have a seat, right here," the little guy said, pointing at the bench.

"What did I do wrong?" I demanded.

"Nothing."

"I don't want to sit down. It's wet and—"

"Sit!" the bigger cop ordered, and he put a hand on my shoulder. I thought about fighting back, maybe even making a break for it—instead I let him push me to the seat.

"Tell me, why did you mention jumping?" he asked.

"I mentioned *not* jumping," I tried to explain.

"I know what you said, but why would you even have thoughts like that to begin with?"

"I don't know," I said, and I shrugged. "I guess it was because Boomer was talking to me about jumpers."

"Boomer? Boomer Williams?"

"Yeah. You know Boomer?"

Both cops burst into laughter. That wasn't the reaction I'd expected, but I liked it a lot better than the angry expressions.

"I don't think there's a cop on the whole force who doesn't know Boomer," the little cop said.

"Who do you think we turn to when we have to find a body that went into the river? You tell him where it went in, or over the Falls, or where it disappeared under, and he'll tell you where it will most likely end up—even if it does take a couple of days to surface."

"Man, I wish I knew my way around my garage the way he knows his way around the river," the little cop said. "Now, how do you know Boomer?"

"I work for him."

"At the museum?"

I nodded. I didn't mention that I hadn't actually started working for him yet.

"I guess that explains it," the little cop said.

I wasn't sure what it explained but I wasn't going to ask.

"You're here because you're a junkie for the Falls. You must be, or you wouldn't be working at the museum."

I didn't say anything. If that explanation made them happy, then it worked for me.

"You had us worried, kid," the big cop said. "We thought you might be a jumper yourself."

"I wasn't going to—"

"We know, we know," he said, cutting me off. "We just have to be careful, that's all. Do you know how much paperwork there is to fill out if somebody jumps during our shift?"

"Does that happen a lot?" I asked.

The two cops exchanged a look. "That's one piece of information you're not going to get from us."

"Yeah," his partner said. "That's one of those numbers they really don't advertise. Now, why don't you go home?"

"Sure . . . thanks."

"And I don't want to see you even close to the gorge any more tonight," the little cop said. "By the way," he asked, "what's your name, kid?"

"Jayson Hunter."

"Leanne Hunter's boy?"

"Yeah, that's my mother."

His face broke into a big smile. "I went to school with your mother. One of the nicest people you'd ever want to meet. Your father was a pretty good guy, too."

"You knew him?"

"I did . . . not from school, though . . . he was a few years older than me. Your dad was a bit wild but a good guy, especially to his friends, and he had lots of those. Shame about the accident. Long time ago now. You tell your mother that Bobby Watson says hey, okay?"

"Sure, I'll do that."

I probably should have been glad that he knew my mother—it probably meant I was a whole lot less likely to get hassled in the future. But instead I just felt that small-town, everybody-knows-your-business feeling—the one that said no matter what I did, or who I tried to be, I was always going to be the kid with the alcoholic mother and the loser dad who took off with the circus and died in a motorcycle accident.

"You need a ride home, Jayson?"

CHAPTER NINETEEN

"MOST OF THIS JOB IS REAL EASY," Boomer said. "Like with this cash register. You scan in the items and it does all the addition. The customer gives you money, you punch in the amount, and the cash register tells you how much to give 'em back in change. Practically idiot-proof."

"We'll see about that," Timmy said. He made it sound as though he was taking that as a personal challenge.

"Probably the most important thing to remember is to never put the customer's money into the till until after the transaction's done."

"Huh?" Timmy asked. I was glad he was there to ask the questions I felt too stupid to ask.

"Let's say the customer gives you a ten-dollar bill. You don't put it in with the other bills in the cash register. You put it right here," he said, tapping the top of the money drawer. "And you only put it in the register after you've counted out the change and he's happy with the amount. Some people will try and argue that they gave you a twenty-dollar bill or even a fifty. When they do that, you just point down to the bill. That's the end of the argument most of the time. If they keep making a big fuss, we have one other thing we can do."

"Kick 'em out?" Timmy asked.

"Go to the video," Boomer said. He pointed up to a camera mounted on the wall above the cash register. "Every transaction is recorded."

"That's like the casino," I said.

"That's where I got the idea."

"Do people try to do that a lot?" I asked. "Complain about the change?"

"More than you'd think. Some are just confused— an honest mistake. But most of them are trying to cheat you. I hate cheats. Nobody is gonna come into my business and cheat me. By the same token, nobody is going to come in here and get cheated . . . or shortchanged. Not by a dollar, not by a quarter, and not by a penny."

I suddenly felt guilty. I wasn't going to do that, but I knew about how tourists were treated in other places—places like the arcade.

"I've lived my life trying to do the right thing. Maybe it hasn't made me super-rich, but people see me as a man they can trust. I treat people fair. When I say something, I mean it. I don't go back on my word. And this business is an extension of me, and while you two work here, you are as well. Do you think you can live up to that?"

"Yeah," I said immediately. Timmy didn't answer.

"Timmy?" Boomer asked.

"I . . . I have to tell you something, man. I really want this job. It's just that I . . . I made a mistake . . . before I knew you really . . . before you offered us the job."

Timmy, just shut up, I thought. It was a big enough mistake taking the T-shirt, confessing to it was just plain stupid.

"The other day I took—"

"A T-shirt," Boomer said, cutting him off. "You stuffed it down your pants."

"You knew?"

"You think the camera behind the cash register is the only one in the store? There are cameras hidden in the ceiling in every corner. The monitors are back in my office."

"You knew, and you still offered me a job?" Timmy asked. He sounded as confused as I felt.

"I didn't know about it until I came back and saw the tapes . . . *after* I'd already offered you guys the jobs."

"But after you'd seen it, you were still gonna let me work here?" Timmy asked. "After you knew I'd scoffed something from you?"

"I had my doubts about how bright it was to still have you work here." He reached over and put a hand on Timmy's shoulder. "Now I don't. I'm proud of you."

"Of *me*? You're proud because I stole from you?"

"Course not. It's what you did after that. That took a whole lot of guts, kid. Now I know I can trust you."

"You can! Believe me, you can!"

"Do I have your word on that?" Boomer asked.

"Of course!"

Boomer reached out his hand and he and Timmy shook.

"You know that when I offer my hand and my word I'd rather die than do something different," Boomer said. "So don't go offering your hand and your word unless you mean the same. Understand?"

"I understand."

"Do you?" Boomer asked. He was still holding on to Timmy's hand. His expression was dead serious and his eyes were bright and sharp. He didn't seem old at all anymore. He seemed strong and powerful.

"I understand. I promise."

"Good." Boomer released his hand. "Now, let's keep moving. There's lots of things I still gotta show you about stocking the shelves, selling admissions, discount tickets. Lots of things. Say, are either of you boys any good with tools?"

"Not me, but Jay is," Timmy said.

Boomer nodded his head. "I should have figured. Your grandfather and great-grandfather were both trained carpenters."

"I didn't know that."

"You don't seem to know much about them, do you?"

I didn't answer.

"I'm gonna be doing some carpentry work to make this new display for your great-grandfather. There's gonna be pictures, newspaper articles, eyewitness reports. It's gonna be pretty sharp. How does that all sound?"

"Good, I guess."

"People are gonna learn a whole lot about your great-grandfather. I think he hasn't been celebrated nearly as much as he should."

"How about you?" I asked.

"How about me what?"

"How come there isn't a display about you?"

He snorted. "Wouldn't it look a little strange for me to make a display about myself?"

"Well … couldn't it just be about those guys who risked their lives to save people?"

Boomer didn't answer, but he didn't snort either. "Interesting idea. Do you boys have any other ideas?"

"Um … not that I can think of … right now," I said.

"I don't usually have any ideas," Timmy said. "At least, ideas that don't get me in trouble."

Boomer laughed. "How about both of you think about things a little. You've probably noticed that business isn't the best it could be. This place could use some new ideas—especially ones that wouldn't get *me* in trouble. Okay?"

"Sure, I guess."

"Good. I'm gonna go and get us some coffee and donuts. I'll be back in fifteen minutes. You boys are in charge."

Timmy and I exchanged worried looks.

"You'll do fine. How much do you think you can do wrong in fifteen minutes?"

"Is that a challenge?" Timmy asked.

Boomer chuckled and shook his head. He grabbed his hat and walked out.

I looked over at Timmy. "Man, you should have seen your face when he mentioned that T-shirt."

"It's not my face I was worried about." He held up his hand. "When he shook my hand he nearly crunched the bones. He might be an old man but I wouldn't want to get him mad at me. I'm pretty sure he could mop the floor with both of us."

"Let's just not find out, okay?"

"Don't worry about me. You got my word on it."

I had been a little worried, but not now. Boomer wasn't the only one who always kept his word. Timmy could be a flake sometimes, but he was also somebody who could be counted on.

CHAPTER TWENTY

I SHIFTED FROM FOOT TO FOOT, anxiously waiting—hoping she'd arrive soon, but hoping even more that she wouldn't arrive at all. A car turned onto the street. I recognized it immediately as belonging to Mrs. Bayliss. As it got closer and slowed down I could see she'd already picked up Timmy. He gave me a big wave from the passenger seat. Mrs. Bayliss pulled to the curb and stopped. I opened the back passenger door and jumped in.

"Hey, Jay!" Timmy said.

"Hi . . . hi, Mrs. Bayliss."

"Glad you're ready and waiting. We don't have much time."

I snapped on my seat belt and she started away.

"Is it far from here?"

"Not far, but is anything in the Falls that far from anything else?" she asked.

"I guess not, really."

"Of course, it certainly has gotten a lot bigger since I grew up here. This used to be such a tiny little town, really not much more than a village, and everybody knew everybody . . . and everybody's business."

"Sounds about the same now," Timmy said.

"Not really. There are new suburbs, lots of people who commute—some travel hours to get to work. There's more than just the two high schools, and people are aware of the bigger world—they travel, they go off to university, they move to other places."

"I don't know anybody who moved away," Timmy said.

"Well, lots of us do stay here," she told him. "Like me, and your father, Timmy. But most people in most places stay where they were born. Or if they do move away, like Jay's mother, they come back."

"I'd like to move away," I said.

"You probably will. At least to go to university. You are planning on going to university, aren't you?"

"I don't know," I answered. Maybe I didn't have the marks. Maybe I didn't want to go.

"Is money a concern?" she asked.

"Isn't it always a concern?" I asked.

"I guess it is. I just hope you know that there are scholarships and loans. Some people even join the military and they pay for your university."

Timmy started giggling. "Man, I can't picture you in the army."

"Me? What about you? They'd have you in front of a firing squad before you finished basic training."

"That's no problem for me. I ain't got no thoughts of university. I'm just hoping to finish Grade 11 . . . in less than three years."

"But you are hoping to graduate, right?" Mrs. Bayliss asked.

"Where there's life there's hope . . . why, don't you think I can?"

"I think you work very hard at not working. At being the clown. At setting low expectations."

"Sounds about right," Timmy said.

"Sounds just plain *wrong*. You have potential for better. You both have such potential. That's one of the saddest things about teaching—seeing people who could be so much more, but choose to waste their opportunities."

"Could you tell me a bit more about this meeting?" I asked, changing the subject. I wasn't there for a guidance session.

"I could tell you, but it would be easier to show you." She pulled the car off to the side of the road in front of a pizza parlour. "We're here."

"We're meeting in the pizza joint?" Timmy asked.

"We're meeting in the office *above* the pizza place."

We got out of the car. "Are we late?" I asked, looking at my watch.

"A couple of minutes, but that's okay. They can't start without me, since I'm leading the meeting." She

"No, I'm okay to walk."

"Okay, then. Go straight home."

"I promise." And I walked away before anybody could ask me any more questions.

opened the door leading to the stairs. There were people—kids—sitting on the steps, laughing and talking.

"Sorry I'm late!" Mrs. Bayliss sang out.

They all stood up, making a little path up the middle of the stairs to allow Mrs. Bayliss to pass by. Timmy and I waited at the bottom while everybody else trudged up. Timmy started to follow and I grabbed him by the arm.

"You sure you want to do this?" I asked.

"They got snacks," he said. "Come on."

By the time we reached the top of the stairs everybody else had gone inside. I pushed open the door. They were already taking seats around a big table. There were ten or fifteen people, and after they'd settled in, the only two empty seats were at the end. Timmy and I took those two spots. I looked around the table. Fourteen kids—nine girls and five boys. All teenagers. A couple younger than us, a couple older, but most around our age. I knew three of them and recognized another three from around—either school or the neighbourhood.

"You've probably noticed that we have a couple of new faces at the table," Mrs. Bayliss said. "I'm sure some of you know them already, but for the others, how about we let them start off the introductions tonight. First names only."

"Sure," Timmy said. "I'm Timmy."

"Good to meet you, Timmy," the girl beside him said, and the others mumbled out similar greetings.

I introduced myself next and was greeted the same friendly way.

After I introduced myself, the girl sitting beside me introduced herself, and then the girl beside her, and we went around the table. Everybody seemed friendly—a familiar kind of friendly. The same sort of friendly I'd seen at AA meetings. That was what I'd figured it would be like. But how long was this meeting supposed to be? Didn't really matter, I had no choice but to sit there and take it. Of course, that didn't mean I was going to *say* anything. Matter of fact, I was going to work as hard as I could to not even *hear* anything. If this was like the AA meetings, it was just going to be a bunch of people whining and complaining.

"So, does anybody have anything they want to talk about this week?" Mrs. Bayliss asked.

People started babbling on about how their week had gone. It was the usual sort of conversations you'd expect from a bunch of teenagers—movies they'd seen, part-time jobs, arguments with boyfriends or girlfriends or parents, things they were going to do. It seemed like a bunch of them did a lot of things together. But on top of that there was the occasional flash of AA talk. About parents who were dry, parents who were still drinking. And then one of the girls started to cry.

"Becky, what happened?" Mrs. Bayliss asked.

Another girl got up and put her arm around Becky. I suddenly went from uncomfortable to *very* uncomfortable. I didn't want to be there to watch some stranger cry.

"It's my father . . . he started drinking again." Becky started to really sob, and a second girl got up and wrapped her arms around her as well.

Timmy got out of his chair. He wasn't going to hug her as well, was he? He started toward the door. Man, he was going to leave and—he stopped at the table and grabbed a Coke! He was getting himself a drink! Unbelievable! Then he walked back over and knelt down beside Becky.

"Here, take this, take a sip and then another," he said. "It'll slow down the sobbing."

She looked up at him. "Thanks." She sniffed and took the Coke from him.

Timmy patted her on the arm and then returned to his seat. He gave me a little smile as he passed. Knowing Timmy the way I did, he might have been being nice like that because he figured it would help him pick her up later—she was kind of cute—or it might really have just been him being supportive. Timmy was that way . . . at least when he wasn't being a donkey.

"It's just . . . just that he started drinking . . . and I was trying so hard," Becky said.

"What do you mean, you were trying?" another girl asked.

"You know, helping around the house, making meals, trying to make sure everybody was happy."

"And you think he started drinking because you didn't make things good enough?" that same girl asked.

"Well . . . not completely . . . but if I had only—"

"Stop right there!" a boy ordered. He stood up. "Your father didn't start drinking again because you didn't clean the house, or make the right meal. He started drinking because he's an alcoholic. It isn't your job to take care of *him*. It's his job to take care of *you*!"

She started sobbing even harder. He shouldn't have yelled at her. She was having it tough enough already without him giving her a hard time.

"Cody's right," a girl named Desiree said. "It's not your fault he started drinking again, just like it wasn't your fault that he drank in the first place."

"It's not your fault," one of the girls still hugging her said. "It's *not*."

"Becky is still new to our program," Mrs. Bayliss said. "She doesn't fully understand how it's easy to blame yourself for your parent's drinking problem."

"How could she?" the boy who'd started it all said. "She's only been here a few weeks. It took me a few years, and sometimes I *still* feel responsible, like it's my job."

"That's a good point," Mrs. Bayliss said. "How many people here still sometimes feel like it's their job to keep their parent or parents dry?"

Everybody in the room raised their hand, including Timmy. Reluctantly I did the same. It wasn't that I necessarily felt that way, but I didn't want to be the only one who hadn't lifted his hand.

"How many people feel guilty and responsible?" she asked.

Guilty and responsible for what? I wondered, but I raised my hand along with everybody else. This was getting repetitive. Couldn't we just go back to watching Becky cry?

"How many people here feel like it's their *job* to take care of their parents?"

I felt a shiver shoot up my spine. I *did* feel like it was my job. I raised my hand along with everybody else. It *had* been my job to take care of my mother, for years.

"And finally, how many people feel angry about that?"

My hand shot up into the air, faster than anybody else's.

CHAPTER TWENTY-ONE

I BRUSHED MYSELF OFF, trying to dislodge some of the dust and dirt that my clothes had picked up from all the dirty old boxes and bins. I coughed long and loud. There was a terrible taste in my mouth, and I could almost feel the dust coating my lungs. I guess I should have been more worried about that.

I'd spent the better part of the morning cleaning out the storage room at the museum. There were boxes and crates and containers that looked as though they hadn't been moved or stirred or disturbed for a long time. Years. Decades. Maybe centuries.

Boomer had mentioned that we could do that if we had time. And we had time, all right. Hardly anybody had come into the museum—hardly anybody had come in during any of the five shifts we'd worked— and I couldn't think of anything worse than just sitting around and doing nothing. It was better to be busy. At least, that's what I thought. Timmy disagreed. He figured there was nothing much better than sitting around, doing nothing, and getting *paid* for it. He'd joked around that this was the job he'd been preparing for his entire life.

I needed a break. A break and a Coke. I left the storage room. The museum was empty except for Timmy—who was still sitting where I'd left him two hours earlier, behind the counter, feet up, staring at some videos.

"Whoa, what happened to you?" Timmy asked as I emerged.

"Work can get you sweaty and dirty," I said. "Not that you'd know anything about that."

"I know enough to avoid it," he joked.

"Where's Boomer?"

"Out at the ticket booth."

"Have there been many customers?" I asked.

"Three."

"I'm not even sure why he sits out there," I said.

"I think he just likes sitting in that booth with his paper and his coffee, reading and watching the people stroll by. It's sort of like sitting by the window at the Donut Hole, except he doesn't have to share it with anybody else."

"So you've both just been sitting around doing nothing while I've been working?" I said.

"Doing *nothing*?" Timmy asked, as though he was hurt by my suggestion. "I've been doing plenty."

"Plenty of what?" I demanded.

Timmy tapped a finger against the side of his head. "Thinking. Deep thoughts."

"Yeah, right!" I snapped. "And what deep thoughts have you been thinking?"

"Mainly about that meeting last night."

"The Alateen meeting?"

"Did we go to some other meeting that I've completely forgotten?"

"I just wish I could forget that one. What a complete waste of time," I said.

"Is that really what you think?" he asked.

"Sure. What did you think of it?"

"I liked it. Donuts and pop form two of my favourite food groups."

"I didn't mean the food."

"The girls were good, too. I think I made a smooth move on that Becky girl when I brought her that pop, don't you?"

"I wasn't talking about the girls, either."

"You're interested in the *boys*? Man, I had you wrong all these years. I had no idea that you swung from the other side of the—"

"Timmy, shut up!"

He laughed.

"I mean what people were talking about," I said. "It was stupid."

Timmy shook his head. "I thought there was some good talk."

"What exactly did you think was so good?"

"Lots of things were good, although a lot of it didn't make much sense to me—at least at first."

"And it does now?" I asked.

"It would to you, too, if you'd stop cleaning out storage rooms and spend more time thinking . . . deep thoughts."

"Yeah, right. So what makes sense to you now?"

"Mainly that part about feeling responsible and guilty."

"Do you feel responsible for your father drinking?" I asked.

"When they first said all of that I thought they were crazy. Why would I feel like it's my fault? He's the one drinking the stuff. It's his fault, not mine. And then I started thinking. Sometimes I *do* feel like I should be able to stop him, but I just haven't figured out how, and if I was smarter or better then maybe I could—"

"Everybody feels like that sometimes," I said, cutting him off. "But it's wrong. It's the person who's drinking that's to blame. Nobody else. Period."

"I know that here," Timmy said, again touching a finger to his head. "But sometimes not here," he said, touching his stomach. "Sometimes I still wonder."

"Well then just stop wondering. Been there. Done that. You're the kid. Your father is the adult. I learned that from all the AA stuff my mother spouts off about."

Timmy chuckled. "Aren't you the one who's always saying that AA stuff is just garbage?"

"*Most* of it is. But occasionally something that they say makes sense. Occasionally. It's like the law of averages, you say enough and eventually something you say will be right."

"That's why I talk so much," Timmy said. "I'm trying to increase the odds. But some of the stuff they talked about last night . . . like feeling angry. There are times I'm so angry at my father that I'd like to take a baseball bat and part his hair in a whole new way." He paused. "I guess it's different for you, though."

"What do you mean?"

"Because your mother doesn't drink anymore, so you aren't angry at her."

I didn't answer right away. I guess I shouldn't have been angry with her anymore. She had stopped. It was just that I still felt that way sometimes. Maybe it was more about what used to be than what was now. That was stupid. Being angry wouldn't change the past. Nothing changed the past.

"Do you ever worry that she'll start drinking again?" Timmy asked.

"No . . . not really . . . not anymore . . . at least, not much."

"That's one advantage I have with my father. He'd have to *stop* drinking before I could worry about him *starting* again. At least he's predictable."

"My mother's not going to start again," I said, defending her. "I know she isn't."

"Don't get me wrong, man, I don't think she will. I'd trade places with you in a second. Actually, I was wondering . . ."

"Wondering what?"

He shook his head. "Never mind. It's not important."

"Whenever somebody says that something isn't important it usually is. What is it?"

"Okay . . . I was just thinking . . ." he said, but he didn't continue at first. "You know things aren't easy with my father." He paused. "Sometimes it's so hard that I don't think I can live with him anymore."

"Where would you go?"

"I was thinking . . . I was wondering if maybe I could . . . if I could . . ."

"Stay with me and my mom?"

Timmy nodded.

I put a hand on his shoulder. "You don't even have to ask. You always have a place to go, man, you should know that without even asking. Anytime. I don't care if it's two in the morning, you just come knocking on the door and it'll be open for you."

"Thanks. Do you think your mother would be okay with that?"

"You gotta be joking. The only problem is she might never let you leave."

Timmy smiled. "I might just take her up on that." He paused again. "But really, I can't."

"Why not?"

"I need to stay at home. It's not like my mother is coming back. Somebody's got to be there. My old man wouldn't last a month on his own."

"It's not your job to take care of him."

Timmy started laughing. "I know that. I was putting you on. Obviously you did get something from the meeting yesterday. Maybe there are a few things you've learned."

"What I continually learn is that you're an incredible goof. If you move in, then *I'm* moving out."

"Great! Then I can get your room." Timmy started laughing again.

"How about if we get back to work?" I suggested. "Oh, wait a second, *I* could get back to work. You could *start* working."

"I have been doing something work-related. You think I've been watching MTV?" he asked, pointing up at the video screen. "Check this out."

Timmy took a tape and shoved it into the VCR mounted on the wall.

"What is it?"

"This is actual footage of somebody going over the Falls."

He powered up the TV and it flickered to life. A group of men was unloading a large, white, cylindrical object off the back of a truck. There were ten or twelve guys, and they looked as though they were struggling under the weight and the size of the object.

"That's the barrel," Timmy said. "Although it looks more like a small spaceship."

"That barrel looks familiar," I said.

"It should. It's sitting right over there."

I turned around. There it was—the same barrel as in the video—in the corner of the room.

"Here, let me fast-forward to the good part."

Timmy aimed the remote at the TV and the images started racing forward. He stopped. "Now watch."

"What exactly am I watching?" I asked as the image on the screen rolled rapidly around and around.

"You're watching the camera that's *inside* the barrel taking a picture through the porthole," Timmy explained.

"Inside?" I exclaimed.

There was a rush of trees and bushes and grass as the camera rolled around and around.

"That's the barrel rolling down the slope and toward the water," Timmy explained.

Then there was a sudden drop and water started flowing and splashing all around, and spinning like the inside of a washing machine. Finally the barrel must have settled into the water and it began rocking back and forth.

"Here it goes," Timmy said.

I watched in awe as the camera—the barrel—suddenly plunged over the lip of the Falls . . . and then the camera went blank. Timmy clicked off the TV.

"Wow," I gasped. My whole body felt tingly.

"Pretty amazing, huh?" Timmy asked.

"Yeah . . . amazing."

"I was reading about this guy."

"You were reading?" I asked, sounding surprised.

"I know how to read, you know. Most of the time I just have better things to do. Today, reading was better than cleaning out the storage room. So do you want to hear?"

"Shoot."

"His name is Dave Munday. You were watching the second time he tried to go over the Falls."

"The second time . . . that's right, he's the guy that tried four times, isn't he?"

Timmy nodded. "The first time they put the barrel into the water too far upstream and the hydro authorities had time to reroute the water supply."

"Reroute?"

"Depending on the time of day, more than half of the water goes into the hydro-generating stations and not over the Falls," Timmy explained. "They saw the barrel coming and diverted the water supply. The water level dropped and the barrel got grounded. The second time he made it. That's what you saw in the video."

"Man," I said. "It would take incredible guts to go in once, but to go in twice would be something else."

"Not twice. *Four* times. Remember?"

"Yeah, of course. What happened the other times?"

"The third time his barrel got stuck, grounded at the very edge of the Falls. They finally had to get a crane to lift it out."

"And the fourth time he went over again, right?"

"Three years later. Inside a steel ball."

"I can't believe anybody could go into that water four times. He's got to be the bravest man in the world."

"You know what makes him even braver?" Timmy asked. "He can hardly swim, and he has a fear of water."

I burst out laughing. "You're joking, right?"

He shook his head. "And he lives not far from here."

"I betcha that Boomer knows him," I said.

"No bet. Boomer knows everybody who has anything to do with the Falls, so he's gotta know the first person in history to go over the Falls twice."

"That's something that nobody else will ever do," I said.

"Wrong again, my friend. He was the first, but not the last. There was another guy named Steve Trotter. Two years after Munday did it, he went over the Falls for the second time. And this time he was in a barrel with somebody else."

"A two-person barrel!" I gasped.

"It was the second two-man barrel, but this one was different because his partner was a woman named Lori Martin. She was only the second woman to ever go over. The first since Annie Taylor started the whole thing ninety years before."

"This is all unbelievable," I said. "And I don't mean the part about people going over the Falls—I mean you actually *knowing* all this stuff."

"I'm not stupid, you know," Timmy said.

"I never said you were stupid . . . although many people would disagree. I'm just surprised you've taken such an interest in all of this."

"Why shouldn't I? We're working here, so I might as well know about it."

I turned around. Out of the corner of my eye I had caught sight of movement through the front window. A bus had slowed down and stopped right in front of the museum, blocking the entire window. It was a gigantic tour bus, and the writing on the side was in English and what I figured was Japanese. The big door opened, and people started bouncing down the steps. There were lots and lots of them. They just kept coming—Japanese tourists, all sporting cameras around their necks.

"I think you're going to get a chance to show off your new knowledge. Do you speak much Japanese?" I asked.

CHAPTER TWENTY-TWO

THE FRONT DOOR OPENED and a virtual wave of Japanese tourists washed into the store, flooding into every open space. There were men and women and kids, all tiny and well dressed, and each of them had a camera or two strung around their neck. The air was filled with laughter and loud conversations— conversations in Japanese. And then they started to take pictures. Bursts of flash filled the air.

"Look at 'em all," Timmy whispered. "There must be a hundred of them."

"Not that many, but there are a lot."

I stood back and watched. They swarmed around the displays, taking pictures of the barrels, themselves with the barrels, individual shots, and group shots. A number of them scanned the room with video cameras so that every little detail would be captured. People in the Falls always made fun of the tourists in general, and the Japanese tourists in particular. The joke was that they spent so much of their holiday time looking through the viewfinders of their cameras that they didn't ever see the Falls except through a viewfinder.

"Picture, picture?" a man asked as he held up his camera and thrust it toward Timmy.

"You want me to take your picture?" Timmy asked, mimicking taking a photograph.

The man nodded his head enthusiastically and Timmy took the camera. The tourist then pulled over a woman and the two of them posed, with gigantic smiles plastered on their faces.

Timmy aimed the camera. "I hope this works," he said to me. The camera flashed and clicked.

Both the man and the woman nodded and bowed. Timmy handed him back his camera, and then the woman held out hers.

"You want me to take one with yours as well?" Timmy asked. He was talking slower and louder, as if somehow they'd be able to understand him if he spoke that way.

In answer she pressed her camera into his hands. She called out and another two women rushed to her side to pose. As soon as Timmy took that picture he was handed another camera, and then another. He had apparently found a new job. I edged away before anybody else could ask me to do the same.

In between snapping pictures, the tourists were snapping up things off the shelves: T-shirts, snow-globes, little statues, videos, and lots and lots of postcards. Basically, if it had a picture of the Falls on it, they wanted it. I just hoped I could remember how to use the cash register.

There was a loud clapping sound. I spun around, and everybody stopped talking. Every eye was aimed at a man standing by the door. Boomer was at his side. The man started to speak in Japanese in short, loud, powerful bursts. Nobody else spoke. They watched, silently, nodding their heads. I got the feeling that he was like their teacher and they were his obedient little students.

He gestured toward Boomer and barked out a few sentences. Suddenly Boomer was bathed in the light of dozens and dozens of flashes. People crowded forward. The guy must have told everybody who Boomer was, about his history as a riverman. Boomer patiently began posing for pictures.

And then Boomer began to speak—in Japanese! I certainly hadn't expected that. Timmy and I exchanged surprised looks. I figured he must have learned a few words so that he could say hello and be polite. But he didn't stop after just a few words. He kept talking, and the tourists all nodded along with him. A number of people thrust their hands into the air. Boomer motioned to one of the men at the front and he started to say something, and then Boomer said something back. Was he answering a question? Person after person spoke and Boomer responded. I wanted to know what he was saying, what they were asking, but the only Japanese words I knew were *sushi* and *kimono*.

Without warning, Boomer turned in my direction and gestured. He said something, and while of course I didn't understand what he was saying, I did hear my name spoken among all those meaningless words. The tourists suddenly swung around as one toward me, and I was blinded by the flashes of their cameras.

"Boomer!" I called out. "What did you—?"

"I told 'em about your great-grandfather!" he yelled back. "They all want to have their pictures taken with you because your great-grandfather went over the Falls."

In ones and twos and small groups they began crowding around me. I felt stupid standing there, towering head and shoulders above most of them, while they took turns taking my picture, flashes bursting until my eyes were starry. Timmy was still behind the counter. He had a gigantic grin plastered across his face, as though my misery was giving him a good laugh.

Boomer walked over to my side. "Just smile and pretend you're enjoying yourself."

"Pretend I can do, but it's not so easy."

"Could be worse. You're just gonna stand here and have your picture taken, but Timmy's gonna have to work the cash register."

I looked over at Timmy and gave *him* a smile.

AFTER WHAT SEEMED like a million photographs, and a million smiles and bows and nods to go along with them, the tourists started filtering out of the museum. The tour guide, who spoke some English, thanked me and pumped my hand and bowed. He chased out the last members of the tour and they boarded the waiting bus—leaving behind an empty room and a silence almost as overwhelming as the noise that had preceded it.

"Well, boys, you done good," Boomer said. "Here." He handed Timmy and me a twenty-dollar bill each.

"What's this for?" I asked.

"A gratuity from the tour guide."

"You mean a tip?"

"Exactly. He was pleased with how you boys treated his tour. Taking pictures and being in the pictures and being so friendly."

"They were nice. I just wish I could have spoken to them. Do you think you could teach me some Japanese?"

"It would be my pleasure!" Boomer replied.

"When did you learn to speak Japanese?" I asked him.

"Long time ago. Although, to be honest, I don't speak it that well."

"Sounded pretty good to me," Timmy said.

"And just how would you know if I spoke it good?" Boomer asked.

"I guess I wouldn't," Timmy admitted. "How did you learn it to begin with?"

"Didn't have much choice," Boomer said with a shrug. "I spent a year in Japan."

"What were you doing there?" I asked.

"I was part of a worldwide tour . . . a daredevil show. You know, tightrope walking, high tower diving, motorcycle jumping ... things like that."

"What did you do?" Timmy asked.

"What didn't I do?" Boomer laughed. "I was young and stupid and figured I was unbreakable. At least, I thought that until I broke a few things. Why do you think I limp?"

"I thought it was because you're old," Timmy replied.

"If you don't watch your mouth, *you* might not get any older, but you will get a limp when I kick your butt across the floor."

"I was just joking!" Timmy exclaimed.

"So was I, son . . . don't worry about it. You're a bit of a smart-mouth, but I like that about you. I was jumping cars on my bike and missed the ramp. Broke twenty-three different bones. On the plus side, I can tell when it's gonna rain. I can feel it right in my bones."

"Is the accident what made you give it up?" I asked.

"That last accident did. I came home to mend and never left again."

If I ever leave, I'm never coming back, I thought, but kept quiet.

Timmy started to giggle.

"What's so funny?" Boomer asked.

"I'm just trying to picture you being young and foolish."

"I was young but I was never . . . well . . . let's be honest, I was downright stupid. I was just lucky enough to outlive the stupid part," Boomer said, and he began to laugh.

"Did you ever think about going over the Falls?" Timmy asked.

Boomer stopped laughing. Maybe this was something that shouldn't have been brought up. "I thought about it."

"But you never tried."

Boomer shook his head. "Some people probably figured I didn't have the guts."

"I don't believe that," I said.

"Me neither," Timmy agreed.

"*Nobody* could ever accuse you of not having the guts. How many times did you risk your life going into the water to pull people out?" I asked.

"More than I care to remember."

"And that girl," Timmy said, "the one you pulled out of the water just before she went over the edge. It makes my spine tingle just thinking about that."

"Sometimes I think the reason I didn't try to go over was because I'd seen too much. Pulled out too many people, dead and alive. Seen what the river can do."

"I think you were too smart to try to go over," Timmy said.

Boomer shook his head. "To just jump into the water is plenty stupid. To go in and live, now that takes lots of brains. Even forgetting about building the barrel, you still need to know where to put it into the water, the times of day and seasons and how they affect water levels, the currents, where the barrel is going to come out down below."

"And you know all of those things, right?" Timmy asked.

"I know the river as well as she'll ever allow anybody to know her."

"Have people ever come to you and asked for your help in going over?" I asked.

"All the time."

"And do you help them?"

"Mostly I help them by talking them out of it. Most of the plans are hare-brained and have no chance of working."

"And if you can't talk them out of doing it?" Timmy asked.

"I try harder."

"And if they still won't listen?" Timmy persisted.

"Then I give 'em some advice."

"So you *do* help them."

"Haven't got any choice. Either way, it's probably gonna be me who pulls them out. Much rather pull 'em out alive and breathing instead of dead and bloated." He paused. "Either of you ever seen a body that's drowned?"

We both shook our heads. Except for my grandparents, all done up in their coffins, I'd never seen anybody dead.

"Not a pretty sight. All swollen and puffy. Unless of course it's been under the water for a while and it starts to rot, or gets bashed and battered by the river and the rocks. Parts can be practically torn off and—"

"I think we get the idea," Timmy said, cutting him off.

"What ends up killing most people is that they didn't prepare their barrel, the craft, right. It's either gonna be a ship that will keep 'em safe or a coffin."

"What about Dave Munday?" I asked, pointing out his contraption.

"That's a fine piece of work. That guy's a skilled craftsman. Give him enough time and money and he could probably build a spaceship."

"Did you help him with his trips over the Falls?" I asked.

"If I had helped it wouldn't have taken him four tries to make two trips over. It was me that pulled him out both times, though."

"Do you know him?"

Boomer nodded. "Quiet man. Very humble. Practically a genius. Hold on, I almost forgot something." Boomer limped off and into his office.

"I know somebody who could build a barrel," Timmy said.

"Who?"

He pointed at me and a shiver went up my spine. "You could do it."

"Yeah, right."

"You could. I know you could," Timmy said.

"Even if I wanted to it would take a whole *lot* of money."

Boomer came back out of his office and walked over to us. "Here you go," he said as he handed me an envelope.

"What is it?"

"The money I owe you. The two thousand dollars for your great-grandfather's barrel."

Timmy smiled. "Two thousand dollars. That's a *lot* of money."

CHAPTER TWENTY-THREE

"COKE?" BOOMER ASKED, offering me a drink.

I put down the hammer. "Thanks."

Boomer pulled up a chair and sat down beside me. "It's starting to really take shape."

"Yeah, I guess it is."

The display—*my great-grandfather's* display—was three-quarters finished. The barrel itself would of course be the centre of the exhibit, but we were building walls to go around it, so we'd have somewhere to put up old photographs and newspaper articles describing the day he went over the Falls. There were eyewitness accounts, and an interview with him right after he was pulled out of the barrel. Still to be installed was a small projection theatre. We had a forty-second film clip that showed my great-grandfather as he was being pulled from the barrel. You could see him coming out, a little shaky and unsteady on his feet, and then raising his hands above his head like a champion—like the champion he was.

The film was old and grainy and in black and white. When Boomer had first showed me the footage I couldn't believe my eyes. Now that I'd watched it two dozen times it still sent a chill up my spine.

It was eerie. Here was this man. Long dead. Somebody I didn't know anything about, even though he was related to me. And here I stood, in the middle of a display—a display *I* was making—that honoured his life. And at the centre of that life was an achievement that only a select few had ever accomplished. Deliberately, bravely, my great-grandfather had denied death and the awesome power of the Falls. He had become something really important in a town where practically nobody became anything. And he was my great-grandfather.

"This is going to be real popular with the tourists," Boomer said.

"We could use the business," I pointed out.

"We've been doing okay."

I snorted. "You could do better." There were some shifts when there wasn't enough business to even pay for Timmy and me to be there.

"Where's Timmy today?" Boomer asked.

"I'm not sure," I said, turning away so that I didn't have to look him in the eye. Timmy hadn't shown up for his shift. He'd asked me to go out the night before and I'd turned him down. I'd been feeling tired. Sleep hadn't been coming easily these days and I knew I had to be up early—we *both* had to be up early—for work.

"This is twice he's missed a shift. In baseball he'd get one more chance and he'd be out."

"He probably has a good excuse."

"He didn't the last time. He's not much of a liar."

"That's because he hasn't had much practice. His father isn't well. Sometimes Timmy has to take care of him." That wasn't a complete lie.

Boomer nodded his head. "His old man's a drunk, right?"

"He's got a problem with alcohol."

"That's what I said, he's a drunk."

"He needs to get into AA, he needs to work through the Twelve Step program," I said.

Boomer snorted. "That's eleven more steps than he needs. You only need one step: Stop putting the bottle in your mouth."

"It isn't that easy. Some people need more help."

Boomer laughed. "Aren't you the guy I always hear putting down that group you and Timmy go to?"

"I don't agree with all of it. It's just that some of the things they say make sense."

The front door opened and two cops walked in. Why were they here and what did they want? My first thought was that it had to have something to do with my mother—was she okay, had something happened to her or—

"You here why I think you're here?" Boomer asked and they nodded.

I didn't know what that meant, but thank goodness it wasn't about my mother—of course it wasn't about her. But what was it about?

"Let me get my coat and boots," Boomer said. He got up and started to walk away, leaving me standing there with my mouth open and my mind empty. He stopped and spun around. "You coming?"

"Me?"

"You see anybody else here?" Boomer asked.

"Where are we going?"

"Down to the river," Boomer said.

"The river . . . you mean . . ."

Boomer nodded.

That could only mean one thing. "And you want me to come?"

"Why not?" he said, gesturing to the display that surrounded me. "This stuff just might be in your blood."

I'D BEEN IN THE BACK of a police car once before, but this was different. I was with Boomer instead of Timmy, and we were their guests, not their prisoners. Timmy and I hadn't really done anything wrong, other than being out too late, and maybe being a bit too drunk, and with no good reason to be where we were. They'd asked us questions and we'd basically not answered. We weren't about to tell them we'd been out at a bush party, trespassing on private property, or admit that we'd been drinking. But when we didn't give them the answers they wanted, they threatened to rough us up. It didn't help that Timmy started to give them attitude—how stupid was that? Two big guys with guns and nightsticks and handcuffs and he starts mouthing off to them. I was pretty sure we were going to get a beating. But we got lucky. Instead of pounding us out they decided to make us pound the pavement. They dropped us off on the edge of town, a long way from home. It was a long, cold walk, but it was sure better than the alternative.

The police car slowed down and then bumped up onto the sidewalk, along a path, and to the edge of the gorge, where it came to a stop alongside a half-dozen other emergency vehicles including a fire truck and two ambulances. All of them had their lights flashing. It almost looked pretty . . . festive . . . like Christmas decorations.

The two officers got out and opened our doors— the back doors didn't have inside handles, they only opened from the outside.

"Thanks, son," Boomer said as he climbed out.

"No problem, Boomer."

"Who's in charge here?" Boomer asked.

"Over there, the Captain."

I trailed behind Boomer as he walked over to a group of men—police, ambulance guys, and firemen, standing at the edge of the gorge. They all greeted Boomer warmly. Everybody seemed friendly, but when Boomer introduced me, I got the feeling that they all wanted to know: *Who is this kid, and what's he doing here?* Nobody said a thing.

"What have we got here?" Boomer asked.

"Male. Went over the Falls about . . ." the officer looked at his watch, "almost four hours ago, but the body hasn't come to the surface yet."

"Horseshoe or American Falls?" Boomer asked.

"Horseshoe."

"Where'd he go in?"

"He jumped in from Goat Island."

Boomer shook his head slowly. "Lots of rocks to get caught behind. The body could be cycling around in the water back there, going round and round like a sock in a washing machine. Could come out in two minutes or two days. Not gonna be pretty when it does." Boomer turned to me. "You don't have to come any farther if you don't want to."

"I'm okay."

He nodded and turned back to the officer. "I'll show you the most likely place for it to pop up."

Boomer limped over to the low stone wall that separated the path from the gorge. There was a sign on the wall that read "Authorized Personnel Only!

Danger!" He climbed carefully over the wall and
started down the steep, uneven path that led to the
river. I hesitated for a split second and then hopped
over after him. I almost expected somebody to try
to stop me, but instead the two officers just trailed
after me.

The rocks were wet and slick and my feet skidded
out from under me. I grabbed the metal railing to
regain my balance.

"Better watch your step," an officer said. "We're
here to pull out one body, not two."

"I'll try to keep that in mind."

I kept one hand on the railing as I hurried to try
to catch Boomer. He was moving fast and I struggled
to close the gap. As we descended into the gorge the
mist got more pronounced until it was so thick it
felt like I imagined it must feel being inside a cloud.
A chill went up my spine just as that old familiar
buzzing started in my head. This was very exciting—
being here, being part of all of this. I was excited and
anxious and scared all at once. It was like I didn't want
to be here, but there was no place else in the entire
world I wanted to be more. I knew that feeling. It was
the same one I got when I was standing on a high
place, or riding my dirt bike too fast, or getting ready
to do something that I figured I *could* maybe do, but
I probably shouldn't even be trying in the first place.
It was a fuzzy, warm sensation in the back of my head.

It happened when I was still on the thin edge of being in control, but just teetering there, thinking that I was just about to lose it, but pulling it back, pulling it back, keeping in control, but just barely.

At the bottom of the path, waiting for us, was a small boat—a motor launch—moored on the rocks. There were two more officers standing beside it.

"Any sign?" Boomer asked them.

"Nothing."

"Might not be for a long time. Come on and I'll show you the spot to watch." One of the officers handed Boomer a life jacket and he passed it to me. He was given a second one and he slipped it on. I did the same, tightening the belt and snapping the buckles into place.

"Who's this?" one of the officers asked, pointing at me, finally asking what I figured they all wanted to know.

"My assistant. I'm getting too old to keep doing this forever, you know. Time to start training a replacement."

My eyes widened in shock. He couldn't be serious, could he?

"Either of you got a rain jacket for the kid?" Boomer asked.

"Sure." One officer reached into the boat, rummaged around, and pulled out a small blue package. He opened it up. It was a plastic rain jacket. He handed it to me and I pulled it on overtop of my life jacket.

Not that it would do much good. The mist had already pretty well soaked me to the bone.

Boomer climbed into the boat. One of them went to offer him a hand and he brushed it away with disdain. I lifted a leg to follow, the boat rocked, and I practically fell in.

"Now *him* you coulda helped," Boomer said, and the two officers burst into laughter.

The rope mooring the boat was untied from the rocks, the engine roared loudly, and the boat backed away from the shore and into the current. The officer at the controls started it moving forward and it bucked over a big wave.

"Circle around!" Boomer yelled out over the engine. "You gotta come around across the face of the American Falls."

The officer at the controls nodded his head in agreement. The boat lurched forward as it powered through the waves, and water splashed over the bow and all over my feet.

I shifted around so I was facing Boomer. "How close are we going to get?"

"You ever been on the *Maid of the Mist?*" he yelled.

"Once. A long time ago. It got pretty close."

Boomer laughed. "It *stops* where we're just gonna *start.*"

That strange, warm, fuzzy buzzing in my head got stronger and louder and hotter.

I spun back around so I was facing the bow again. The boat bounced through the waves. The mist continued to get thicker until we were passing through a dense fog. I couldn't see more than a dozen boat lengths ahead of us. Could the officer see any better than me? I could only hope.

We had to be close now. The sound of the Falls was overwhelming. I could hardly hear the roar of the motor anymore. I turned back around. The one officer was still at the controls, wrestling with the wheel.

Up ahead through the thickening mist I could see—or thought I saw—the outline of the Falls. Then I looked to the side. There was a wall of water off to the left that disappeared into the mist! Instinctively I bounced across the seat to the far side to try to get a bit farther away.

"Sit still!" Boomer yelled in my ear. "You trying to tip us over?"

I grabbed onto the seat with both hands. The boat continued to bounce forward. I did my best to forget what was beside us and what was up in front. Then, through a clearing in the mist, I suddenly saw. Not only were the American Falls beside us, we were steaming straight toward the Horseshoe Falls. My eyes rose up and up and up until all I could see was water.

"To the right! More to the right!" Boomer yelled.

The boat cut over as he'd commanded. What did it matter? We were still headed straight toward the

Falls. The boat bucked even more wildly and there was a roar from the motor. I spun around in time to see that the whole stern of the boat had been bounced out of the water, and the motor was churning away in the air!

"Closer! We have to get closer!" Boomer called out.

I couldn't see how it was possible to get any closer without going right under. The boat pressed forward, fighting hard against the current, bouncing so strongly that I feared I was going to be thrown right out. I dug my fingers in, clasping the bottom of the seat.

"Now cut the motor!" I heard Boomer yell.

I spun around in shock. He couldn't be serious about that.

The faint, high-pitched whine that was the motor stopped. The boat stopped vibrating and started to swing around as it was caught, unable to fight against the current. I braced my legs against the bottom of the boat and reached out until I had my hands anchored to opposite gunwales. The boat spun around until it was pointed away from the Falls. It was pushed by the current and rocked by the waves, but we were definitely moving away from the Falls. I looked back over my shoulder. The wall of water was lost in the mist that it was throwing up. The sound was still overwhelming but it was less deafening. I felt myself starting to relax a little.

"Rocks to the left!" one of the officers yelled.

We hit against the rocks with a loud crack and we spun sideways and rolled around them. The boat kept slowly spinning as we drifted through the mist . . . drifting away from the Falls.

"What are we doing? Why did you have them cut the motor?" I asked.

"I needed to know how the body's gonna drift when it finally does come out. That's why I let the boat drift."

"So because the boat drifted here, the body will too?"

"That's the idea, but not necessarily. Different weight and size. Still, this is the best guess I can make."

"There's the shore, right up ahead!" one of the officers called out.

The boat continued to drift toward the rocky shore. The motor launch ran up against the shore, one of the officers, holding the bowline, jumped out and onto the rocks. He secured the line, and the second officer jumped off and joined him. Together they pulled the boat up onshore, and the bottom scraped noisily against the rocks. Boomer and I climbed over the side and joined them as the two started to walk along the shore, disappearing into the thick mist.

"So we just sit here and wait?" I asked.

"Nope. They've gone up to get some other members of the search and rescue squad. They'll come down, check out the rocks along this stretch, and then *they'll* wait."

"For how long?"

"Minutes. Hours. Days." Boomer squatted down on the rocks. "Might not find it at all. Lots of bodies that go over are never found."

"How can they not find a body?"

"It's a big river, and it leads to an even bigger lake."

There was something I had to ask. "Were you serious . . . about me being somebody you could train to do this . . . somebody who could know about the river? Do you think it could be me?"

"Wasn't really thinking much about it one way or another. Just wanted to make sure that they wouldn't object to you coming along."

"Oh . . . yeah . . . sure . . . I understand." I didn't know whether I should feel disappointed or relieved. Instead I felt both.

"Course, no reason why you *couldn't* be the person. It *is* in your blood. The same blood that flowed through your great-grandfather's veins flows through yours."

His blood *was* in my veins and somehow I *did* feel strangely at home here. I stood there on the rocks, on the edge, the mist swirling around me, and thought about my great-grandfather in that old wooden barrel going over those Falls . . . did he come out around here somewhere?

"It is a high isn't it?" Boomer said.

"Yeah, it was like a roller coaster ride."

"Always gets my old heart pumping faster. Yours?"

"Really fast."

"Adrenalin will do that. Bigger rush than alcohol or drugs ... not that you'd know about that."

"No," I said. "Not really." That was only a partial lie. The alcohol I knew about, but except for a couple of tokes of weed I'd always avoided drugs. "This is a different feeling . . . better."

Boomer nodded. "Better because it's more powerful. A bigger high. A bigger rush. To stand there looking death in the eye and staring it down, not blinking, and surviving. That's the rush. That's why people do it. I can only imagine the rush of going over."

I knew what he was saying was right.

"I saw you the other night, in the middle of the night, out there staring at the Falls," Boomer said.

I felt embarrassed. I hadn't seen him. I didn't know what to say.

"It's all right. I've spent a lot of sleepless nights out there myself. Just staring at the water. Thinking."

"What do you think about?" I asked.

"Lots of things. Life. Death. I guess more about death these days. Wondering if it's really the end. What were *you* thinking about?"

Now I knew what to say but I didn't want to so I remained silent.

"I know what I was thinking about when I was your age," Boomer said. "I was thinking about the river . . . wondering . . . wondering if I could go over the Falls." He struggled to his feet and I offered him a hand. He held on to me. "Is it the same with you?"

I didn't answer.

"Thinking about it is okay. Trying to do something about it is another thing. You don't have any crazy ideas, do you?"

"Nothing crazy," I reassured him.

"Good, because—"

"Boomer!" a voice bellowed out of the mist. "Boomer!"

The two officers reappeared. "The *Maid of the Mist* just radioed in. They spotted a body."

CHAPTER TWENTY-FOUR

"JAY, YOU'VE BEEN EVEN QUIETER than usual tonight," Mrs. Bayliss said, and a couple of other members of the Alateen group nodded or voiced agreement.

I shrugged.

"He's had a pretty rough day," Timmy said, and I shot him a dirty look.

"I'm sorry to hear that," Mrs. Bayliss said.

"Anything we can help with?" one of the girls asked.

I shook my head. "There's nothing anybody can do. It's over."

"What's over?"

"The guy's life," Timmy said. "Jay helped pull a body out of the river today."

I was going to bark something at Timmy but before I could, everybody in the room reacted, all of them asking me questions or making comments at once.

"I didn't do anything. I didn't pull anybody out of the river. I was just there. The police pulled him out."

"Why were you even there to begin with?" somebody asked.

"I went along with Boomer . . . he runs the Daredevil Museum."

"Where me and Jay work," Timmy added. "The police call him in when a body goes over the Falls."

"That's so sad, an accident like that happening," a girl said.

"Probably no accident," another said.

"Was it a suicide?" Timmy asked me.

"I really can't talk about it," I said, shaking my head.

The police had told Boomer, and he'd told me, but he'd made me promise not to say anything. It was confidential. Actually, even if I'd been allowed to talk about it I wouldn't have. Apparently there was a hotel key in the guy's pocket when they pulled him out. That led them to his room . . . and a suicide note. The guy was from somewhere down in the southern States. He'd come all this way up here to kill himself. He had to have passed thousands of places that would have been just as good, but he wanted the Falls. The suicide letter said something about how this was where he and his wife had gone on their honeymoon, and now that she'd left him he wanted to go back to where it had all started.

"Tell 'em about what the body looked like," Timmy said.

"I don't think that would be appropriate!" Mrs. Bayliss exclaimed.

"Why not? I thought we could talk about anything here," a boy said.

"Anything related to alcohol."

"Maybe after the meeting you can—"

"I'm not talking to anybody about it," I said, cutting him off. "I've already talked to one person too many," I said, shooting Timmy a hard look.

The man had been pretty beaten up. His face— what was left of it—was all smashed up, and the top of his head was bashed in so it wasn't round anymore. What was even worse was the body itself. The clothes were almost all ripped off to reveal the grotesquely swollen, whitish-grey flesh. Boomer said that was how a body got when it had been underwater.

"We're almost at the end of our time tonight," Mrs. Bayliss said. "Does anybody have anything else they want to talk about? Anything related to alcohol?"

Nobody had anything to say.

"Then let's call it a night." People got up from their seats. "Jay, could I talk to you for a minute?"

I stopped halfway up and settled back into my seat.

"I'll wait for you downstairs," Timmy said as he walked out with all the others, leaving just Mrs. Bayliss and me in the room.

She walked over and sat down on the table beside me. "Are you okay?"

"As okay as I can be."

"Do you want to talk?"

"What good would that do? It wouldn't bring him back to life, or stop me from thinking about it."

"Sometimes the secret isn't to try to stop thinking about it, but to let it out," she said.

"You know, there was alcohol involved," I said. "There were lots of empty bottles in the hotel room . . . the police told Boomer."

"That doesn't surprise me. I was drunk when I tried to kill myself."

"When you *what*?" I gasped.

"Tried to end my life. Pills . . . an overdose."

"But . . . but . . . you just don't seem like the type to do that."

"Alcohol makes anybody the type. Look, if you decide you need to talk, you just call me. Day or night. Okay?"

"I will. Thanks." I got up. "I'd better go. Timmy's waiting."

I hurried out of the room and down the stairs. Timmy was sitting on the bottom step.

"Come on, let's get going," I said as I bounced past him.

"Slow down!" he called out. "What's the rush?"

I just kept going. Timmy ran to catch up to me.

"Why didn't you tell them about the body?" Timmy asked.

"Like I said, I already told *one* person too many."

"But you said you only told . . . oh, you mean me, right?"

"Good guess."

"So what, are you not gonna tell me things now?" Timmy asked.

"I'll have to stop if you don't learn to shut up sometimes."

"I was just trying to do you a favour," Timmy said.

"How is you shooting off your mouth doing me a favour?"

"Didn't you see the way the girls reacted? Dead bodies are cool."

"Dead bodies are *cold*."

"I was trying to make you out to be a hero so maybe you could get a little action with the ladies. In case you haven't noticed, you ain't doing so well lately."

"And you're doing better?"

"I was last night," Timmy said, and he smiled.

"Yeah, right, and who was the *lucky* lady?"

"You know her . . . at least, I think you know her. Her name is Amber."

"Like that narrows it down. Half the girls in town are named Amber."

"And the other half are called Crystal," Timmy said. "And the third half are called—"

"Timmy, there aren't three halves."

"I was just trying to make a point. But you *do* know this Amber. Amber Commisso."

"You were hanging out with Amber *Commisso?*"

"More like hanging *on* Amber Commisso. She's hot, and more than a little wild, and she likes the Tim-man."

"Are you crazy?" I snapped. "She's Angelo Commisso's little sister and Rudy Commisso's daughter. You mess with her and the next body I help pull out of the river might be *yours.*"

"This isn't an episode of *The Sopranos*, you know," Timmy said. "Nobody's gonna drop me in the river." He started to laugh.

"You're probably right," I said. "They might just put you in one of those machines. You know, the ones they use to crush junked cars at the wrecking yard they own."

Timmy stopped laughing. "Do you really, for a fact, know that they're *connected?*"

"No, but do you really, for a fact, know that they're *not* connected?"

Timmy didn't answer.

"Why take a chance?" I asked.

"Two reasons come to mind . . . man, can that girl ever fill out a T-shirt."

"Timmy, think with your brain sometimes."

"I tried that. It gave me a real sharp pain right there between the—"

"Stop that!" I snapped as I grabbed him by the arm and spun him around to face me.

"Okay, okay, I'll stop seeing her!"

"Good, but that's not what I was talking about. Why don't you stop acting like you're stupid all the time?"

"Who's acting?"

"Cut it out. You're not stupid."

"You obviously didn't see my last report card. Or the one before that. Or the one before that. Or the—"

"I'm not talking about your marks in school," I said. "They *do* suck. But I'm talking about your smarts. I know you could do better in school if you wanted to."

"Couldn't do much worse and still pass."

"If you buckled down and worked you could do *better*."

"First off, you're not my father—you're sober, for one thing, so that's a difference. Second, if *you* buckled down you could get better marks too, so don't go talking to me about it. Third, what difference would it make? I'm just putting in time anyway. I turn sixteen in October and then I can become an official dropout."

"And then what? You gonna get a job at the arcade, or at one of the hotels?" I didn't like to think about Timmy turning into Jack, working a dead-end job and getting his kicks from shortchanging the tourists. I didn't like to think of me ending up that way, either. "Or maybe Boomer would take you on full-time at the museum. Thirty-five hours a week at minimum wage. That'll really add up," I taunted him.

"I got plans."

"Then let me in on them," I demanded.

"My father was a tool and die maker. He still has all his tools and some machines in the garage."

"And he's going to sober up long enough to teach you?" I said mockingly. "The only thing he could teach you is how to become a falling-down drunk!"

"For that I don't need lessons. That's something that's passed on through the genes, like eye colour."

"Timmy, I'm not joking."

"Neither am I. Have you been listening to anything we talk about in those Alateen meetings?"

"Quit it, Timmy. Do you really have a plan?"

He nodded. "My old man's still got connections in the business. He used to be really good . . . respected. He thinks he can get me a job in a machine shop, maybe an apprenticeship, and I can become a tool and die maker too."

"Sorry . . . that sounds good . . . I never knew that's what you wanted to do."

"I don't *want* to do it, Jay. Nobody *wants* to work in a factory. It's just what you become because you gotta become something."

"I guess so. But didn't you ever have something that you really wanted to do?" I asked.

"Yeah. I had dreams of getting inside of Amber Commisso's sweater, but that doesn't look like it's gonna work out."

"Be serious."

"You want serious? Okay, when I was little, really little, and didn't know any better, I wanted to become a pilot."

I laughed before I could stop myself.

"Gee, thanks for being so supportive."

"I'm sorry, it's just that you're afraid of heights," I explained.

"I'm not afraid of heights. I'm just not stupid enough to stand on the brink of a cliff . . . like some people I know. Being in a plane is different. But what are we even talking about any of this for anyway? I'm not gonna become no pilot."

"You could."

"Yeah, right. So what's your big dream? Do you still want to drive choo-choo trains?"

"An engineer doesn't drive——"

"I'm just putting you on, man, I know that. So what do you want?"

"What I really want is to get out of this town. Go somewhere else." I'd had enough of it—enough of people thinking they knew who I was just because they knew something about my mom, or my dad. Enough of being stuck somewhere where no one had any bigger dreams than picking money from tourists' pockets. The roar of the Falls had become like a roaring in my head, pushing me away.

"It's not so bad around here," Timmy said. "It's where we belong."

"Not where I belong . . . and not you, either. We can leave here. We can break free, get to someplace better."

"And just what is your big plan?"

I didn't answer.

"Come on, you demanded to hear my plan. So let's hear yours."

"If I tell you, you have to promise you're not going to say a word. Not to anybody."

"You ask me to keep my mouth shut, then it stays shut."

I nodded. "You're going to think I'm crazy."

"Only one way to find out."

This was probably a mistake, but I'd started it, and saying it out loud was the first step. I took a deep breath. "I think my best chance of getting *out* of the Falls is by going *over* the Falls."

Timmy didn't say anything. The look on his face didn't change. He didn't even blink.

"Did you hear what I said?" I asked.

"I heard you. I'm just not sure what the correct answer is to somebody who just told you his dream is to go over Niagara Falls. And believe me, I've had lots of time to think about what sort of answer I was going to give you."

"Lots of time? What do you mean?"

"You been thinking about this for at least a week, right?"

"Maybe two . . . but how did you know that?" I asked.

"It's like you said, I'm not stupid. I've been listening to the questions you've been asking Boomer. The way you've been studying the stuff about people who went over."

"You've been looking at the books and videos too," I said.

"Looking. You've been *studying* them. And you don't think I haven't seen you out there by the railing, staring out at the river?"

I didn't know what to say. I felt like I'd been caught doing something bad, or wrong. I had been spending a lot of time gazing at the Falls.

"That's where you were last night, right?" Timmy asked. "When I was trying to feel up Amber Commisso, you were down by the Falls."

"For a while," I reluctantly admitted. "Then I went to bed. One of us got up early and went to work today," I said, trying to change the subject.

"Yeah, I sort of slept in."

"Sleep in again, and Boomer's going to can you."

"Whatever."

"No, he really will. You have to take this stuff seriously," I said.

"You're talking about going over the Falls and you want me to get worked up about being fired?" He paused. "This going over the Falls stuff is all just talk, right?"

"Not so much talk as thought."

"But you haven't actually done anything, have you?"

"I haven't built a barrel, if that's what you mean. But I could if I had some help."

"You mean like my help?" Timmy asked. "And just what is it that you think I could do?"

"For starters, I need a place to build it."

"My bedroom is pretty small."

"I was thinking your garage. Your father has lots of tools . . . welding equipment even, right?"

"He has a full workshop in there."

"And if we rearranged things there'd be enough space, right?"

"There's space."

"Maybe I could offer to rent it from him for a month or two."

"That wouldn't work," Timmy said. "If you did that he'd be interested in what was going on out there. Better just to use it and not tell him."

"But what if he does find out?" I asked.

Timmy shook his head. "He doesn't notice anything that doesn't come in a bottle."

"So I can use it?"

"It's yours. What about money? You'll need money to make a barrel," Timmy said.

"I've got the money from Boomer. Plus the money I get from working . . . and the money you get."

"You want me to give up my pay?" Timmy exclaimed.

"Yeah. I was hoping you'd invest."

"Invest? What's that supposed to mean?"

"If you put some money into me building my barrel, then you'll get money back when this works. You saw the way those Japanese tourists acted because my great-grandfather went over the Falls. How do you think they'll react if *I'm* the one that goes over?"

"They'll pay money, lots of money, to get their picture taken with you," Timmy said.

"And there'll be more than that. There'll be appearances on TV shows. And maybe we can shoot video of me going over . . . Who knows, they might even put my face on some plates or something. And you'll get a cut of everything I make. Well?"

"The money-back part is appealing. The helping you to kill yourself part isn't."

"I'm not planning on killing myself. I'm planning how to do it and live."

"Plans go wrong."

"I think I can pull it off. Let me convince you."

"First I got to make a phone call."

"To who?" I demanded, grabbing him as he started to walk away. Was he going to call my mother or Boomer or—?

"I have to call Amber. I've got to cancel our date . . . our double date."

"Double date? Who else were you going out with?"

"You . . . and Amber's little sister, Chantel."

"Man, and you think going over the Falls is dangerous. Make your call, and then we'll talk."

CHAPTER TWENTY-FIVE

I'D TAKEN A LARGE metal wine barrel—the kind they used to store thousands of bottles of wine while it was fermenting—as the basic outer shell of my ship. Despite the washing and scrubbing it still smelled of alcohol. Inside that I'd inserted a fibre-glass storage container. This was the place where I'd be. In between the two layers I was stuffing in insulation. I pushed another piece of pink insulation between the two walls. My arms, right from the tops of my gloves to the sleeves of my T-shirt, were covered in prickles. Whatever was in this insulation was giving me a rash. I shoved the piece as far as I could into the gap. I wasn't looking for the stuff to insulate anything—it was to act as protection, something to absorb the shock if I hit a rock. A direct blow would probably shatter the outer shell of the barrel, no matter what I did, but I figured I could survive a glancing blow if I put in enough padding.

I grabbed another slab of the fluffy pink insulation. Timmy had ripped off fifty pieces from a house that was being renovated a couple of blocks away. At first I'd thought he took way too much, but now I figured I could use another ten or so pieces. I'd talk to him.

I heard the side door open and turned around to see Timmy. His hair was sticking up in a hundred different directions. He looked like he was still half asleep.

"What did you do, sleep here last night?" he asked.

"I slept at home . . . for a couple of hours. Then I woke up with some ideas swirling around in my head. Better to get working on them than to lie there thinking about working. I got this great idea about a better way to secure the door. Let me show you."

"Wait, let me show *you* something."

"Show me you can lock the door first," I said, motioning behind him.

"You expecting a break-in?" Timmy chided me.

"Just lock the door."

He turned back around and used his key to lock it. There were two keys to the garage door. I had one and Timmy had the other. That way nobody—including his father—could just walk in here. As well, we'd covered the back window with foil so nobody could peek in, either.

"So what do you want to show me?" I asked.

Timmy pulled a video camera out from behind his back.

"Where'd you get that?"

"A guy I know. We can have it for a few weeks. I figure we should start taking videos of the construction. I'm just sorry we missed so much already."

"I'm just happy that we've been able to do so much in the last two weeks."

"And then—this is the beauty part—we hook the camera up inside the barrel. We do what Dave Munday did and film you going over the Falls from the inside."

"I don't know if we should do that. It could be a really rough ride. What if the camera gets broken?"

Timmy laughed. "Get real. If you live, the film is worth a fortune. If you die, you're not sweating a broken camera."

"I guess you're right," I admitted. "I could probably rig something up so it would be okay. I just have to surround it with enough padding to—hey, that reminds me, I need some more insulation. Can you get me more of this stuff?" I asked, holding up one of the remaining slabs.

"No problem. There's a couple of houses being renovated. I can't get over all those people moving in and fixing up the old houses around here."

There was a pounding on the door and I jumped in shock. Timmy and I exchanged questioning, worried, wondering looks. Was it his father or—?

"Open the door!"

It was Boomer!

"What do we do?" Timmy whispered.

"Stay quiet . . . maybe he doesn't even know there's anybody——"

"Open the door, Timmy!" he yelled. "I just saw you go in there!"

So much for that plan.

"Go . . . open the door . . . go *out* and see him," I whispered. "He knows *you're* in here, but he doesn't know *what's* in here."

Timmy nodded his head and moved toward the door. I went over and hid behind the barrel.

Boomer pounded on the door again.

"Hold your horses!" Timmy yelled. "I'm coming!"

I peeked around the side of the barrel as Timmy unlocked and opened the door ever so slightly, putting himself squarely in the opening.

"Hey, Boomer, what are you doing here?" Timmy asked, sounding all friendly and innocent. "I'm not supposed to be working today so——hey!"

Timmy bounced back as Boomer pushed past him and into the garage.

"What are you doing?" Timmy demanded.

"It's not what I'm doing, it's what you're doing," he snapped. "Might as well come out of where you're hiding, Jay!"

There was no point in hiding——at least hiding me. I got up quickly and put myself squarely in front of the barrel, like I could block it with my body.

"Nobody's hiding," I said. "I'm right here." I walked toward him. The closer I got to him the more of the barrel I could block.

"We're just going out for breakfast. How about if you drive and I'll treat you?" I suggested.

"Not interested in breakfast," he said. He put a hand on my shoulder and pushed me slightly over to the side. He walked over until he was standing right in front of the barrel.

Boomer put a hand against the metal. He circled around, bending down to look at the bottom, checking it out from all angles. He wasn't just looking at it, he was studying it.

I looked at Timmy and he gave me a "what now?" look. I didn't really have an answer, but I had to come up with something.

"Now you've ruined the surprise," I said.

Boomer turned to look at me. "I hope I'm ruining your *plans*."

"My plan was to build this so it can go in the museum as a display," I said.

Timmy looked completely surprised.

"I was building it so that you could—"

"You never lied to me before so don't start now," Boomer growled.

"I'm not—"

He tapped a finger forcefully against my chest. "I'm not an idiot, and you're no liar, so let's not do this dance. I know what you're doing."

That couldn't be possible. The only person who knew was Timmy, and unless he had said something then Boomer couldn't possibly know. Angrily, I turned to Timmy.

"Don't look at me!" he exclaimed. "I didn't tell him nothing!"

"Didn't need to. I already had it figured out."

"You knew I was building a barrel?" I questioned.

"I knew you were thinking about it," Boomer said, "but I had no idea you were this far along."

"How long have you been suspicious?" I asked, wondering if my mother might be thinking the same thing.

"I started wondering weeks ago. At first I was afraid to ask in case you *weren't* thinking about it and I was putting thoughts in your head. That's one of the reasons I had you come down to the river with me to retrieve that body."

"I don't understand."

"I wanted you to see what the Falls can do to a person. Thought I could put a little fear in you . . . make you think."

"It made me think, but it didn't make me want to turn back."

"It would be smart to turn back," Boomer said.

I shook my head. "I'm not turning back."

"Maybe somebody should *make* you turn back."

I startled. Somebody . . . did he mean him? "Are you going to try to stop me?"

"I might just tell your mother."

"You can't do that!"

"I can. Probably should."

"All right, then go ahead," I said. "Call her . . . that is, if you can honestly say to me that part of you isn't excited by the idea . . . that part of you doesn't wish it was you doing it . . . that you aren't just a little bit interested."

"Doesn't matter if I'm interested or not. What matters is that your blood would be on my hands. Do you really think I'm going to stand by and let you kill yourself?"

"I'm trying to not kill myself. I've thought this through. I've been studying it, planning, working it out." I paused. "I can do it, and if you could help me then—"

"I'm not gonna help you!" he snapped.

"Could you at least look at it?" I asked. I'd noticed him stealing glances at it as we were talking. He wanted to see it. "That wouldn't hurt, would it?"

Boomer didn't answer at first. "I could look at it I guess . . . a little." He walked over and started to examine the barrel.

I nudged Timmy. "Come on," I whispered.

We stood behind him, silently, watching, as he moved all around the barrel, studying it from all angles. Finally, after what had to be five minutes, he turned back around.

"What do you think?" I asked.

"Looking at your barrel I can see where you've been studying Dave Munday's design."

"No point in reinventing the wheel," I said. "That man knew what he was doing."

"Man was a real craftsman. Hard to go wrong following the best."

"I've made some changes to his design, though. Do you want to see my plans?"

"I'd like to see 'em. That way I can tell you if you're just building yourself a shiny coffin."

"And you'll tell me the truth?" I asked.

"I always tell the truth. Too old and ornery to care if somebody doesn't like what I have to say."

"I just don't want you to try to talk me out of it," I said.

"If I think it's got no chance I'm only going to be talking to the authorities and telling them to take the whole thing away."

"What? What are you talking about?"

"It's still against the law to try to go over the Falls. If I tell the Parks Authority and the police what you're working on, they'll be in here in twenty minutes and they'll haul the whole thing away to the dump."

"And you'd do that?"

"I might. I might not. Let me look at the plans first."

"Before you start," Timmy said, holding up his arms, "I'm going to go and get some breakfast. I'm heading over to the Donut Hole and I'll grab some donuts and coffee and bring them back."

"Make mine with lots of milk and six sugars," Boomer said.

"Are you planning on drinking it or eating it?" Timmy asked.

"Just go on and be a good delivery boy and leave me to look at the plans."

Timmy saluted, spun around, and left, leaving the door open behind him. I hurried over and closed it.

"Have you even figured out how you're going to get it to the river?" Boomer asked.

"Not yet. I was just focusing on building it first."

"And where were you planning on putting it in once you got it there?"

"I was thinking the same place Dave Munday did the first time he went over. If it worked for him, it should work for me."

"Not unless you go in at the same time of day, and the same time of year, and the water levels are the same."

"I didn't know that."

"I've forgotten more about that river than you'll ever know," Boomer said. "And in this case, what you don't know might just kill you."

"But with your help, with your knowledge, I'd have a slightly better shot, right?"

"Slightly? With my help you'd have an honest-to-goodness chance of walking away with your . . ." He stopped himself. "Kid your age hasn't lived long enough to know that death is a possibility."

"I know people die."

"Not people . . . *you*." He put a finger against my chest. "If it goes wrong, *you're* dead."

"You've seen the barrel. Look at the plans. I'm not just jumping in. I'm building the best thing I can."

"Half of those who planned and prepared still died. Not great odds. Half of them. Are you willing to roll the dice on your life?"

"With your help I have a better chance of living. You can help me live."

"I can *guarantee* you'll live if I put a stop to it right now."

"I can't stop you from stopping me," I admitted. "*This* time." I paused. "But I'm going to do it. You can have them take away this barrel and the next one I try to build, but sooner or later it's going to happen. You know that."

He didn't answer.

"It *is* in my blood. Help me do it right . . . that's all I'm asking."

He nodded his head slowly. He reached out his hand and we shook.

CHAPTER TWENTY-SIX

IT WAS TIGHT, but almost cozy. The bottom straps —the ones keeping my legs suspended—were starting to hurt. I'd try to adjust those again before I climbed back in. I was suspended, like in a hammock, with three sets of straps: one for my legs, a second for my lower body, and a third up by my shoulders. They held me in place so that I wouldn't be tossed around and smashed against the sides.

I looked at my watch. I'd been inside almost fifteen minutes. We were hoping to—in some small way— simulate what it would be like for me on the big day. There were obvious differences, of course—like the fact that I hadn't dropped hundreds of metres or been tossed around like an egg in a crate. Instead, the barrel was just up on the hoist in Timmy's garage.

The biggest difference, though, involved trying to figure out the time that would be involved. Technically, it could all happen in less than ten minutes. I could be locked inside, be rolled into the river, go over the Falls, pop out, and be pulled from my barrel in less than ten minutes. Or, if things didn't go perfectly, it could be an hour. Or more.

I reached over and put a hand on the oxygen tank. I didn't need it now. The air was still fresh. It was flowing in through the special filter system Boomer had helped me install. Originally I'd put it in backwards. It would have stopped water from flowing *out* of the barrel while letting it flood *in*, drowning me almost instantly. I shuddered. I couldn't help wondering just what would have happened if he hadn't gotten involved. Actually, there was no wondering— I would have been dead. Now, with his help . . . I might still die.

If I was above the water, the filter system would allow air in—like it was now. If I was caught underneath, then I'd have to rely on the oxygen in that tank to keep me alive. How long had Timmy told me the guy at the scuba shop said it would last? Was it thirty minutes or forty? Was it possible to buy a tank with more air?

I was amazed by how quiet it was. The sounds of the world had all been blocked out. I felt relaxed. I thought I could almost go to sleep in there.

I closed my eyes and tried to imagine what it would be like climbing out after I'd gone over the Falls . . . that was only two days from now . . . less than two days. Two days from now, at this time of the day, it would all be over . . . one way or another.

There was a loud, metallic tapping and I was jarred back to reality. My eyes popped open and I looked at the porthole. Boomer's face—all distorted through the thick glass—smiled at me. I gave him the thumbs-up. I heard the sound of the screws being loosened to open up the hatch. It was a slow process—closing the hatch or opening it up again. It had to be that way to make sure that it was sealed tightly enough to keep the water out and keep me safe inside. My only worry was about what would happen if I needed to get out quickly. What if my oxygen was gone? The time it took to undo the hatch could mean the difference between life and death. Again, I wondered if maybe we could get a bigger air tank with a longer capacity. Finally the hatch popped open and a rush of cool air surged in.

"So, how did it feel?" Boomer asked.

"Not bad. I want to adjust the straps around my legs, though. They were starting to dig in."

"Leave 'em alone. Digging in means they're tight. Just add another layer of clothing to protect yourself."

I undid the straps and started to climb out. The hatch was little—deliberately so—and it was a tight fit. Boomer grabbed me by the shoulders and practically hauled me out and onto my feet. I was always amazed by his strength. I guess I should have been grateful. It was Boomer who was going to haul me out at the end, and I might not be conscious to help

him. I could only imagine how strong he must have
been when he was young.

"It's good to know that everything is working," I
said.

"Guaranteed to work . . . as long as it sits in somebody's garage. What happens when it goes over the
Falls and under the water is just an educated guess."

"It's more than that," I argued. "We've done our
homework and—"

"And your filter's now in correctly," Boomer said,
cutting me off.

"Yeah. But we've built it the best way we could. It's
solid . . . don't you think?"

Boomer didn't answer. Instead, he started to walk
around the barrel, peering at it like he was seeing it
for the first time. I followed along behind him as he
ran a hand along its curves.

It certainly wasn't like my great-grandfather's barrel. For starters, it was much bigger—at least five
times as big as his pickle barrel. And instead of wood
it was made of fibreglass, insulation, and metal. The
top wasn't simply nailed on, I had a double-sealed
hatch—solid metal, with a rubber gasket around the
edges to stop any leaks, and a thick, thick glass porthole in the middle to allow me, and the camera, to
see out. It would have been pitch-black for my great-
grandfather. I had the light from that porthole, as well
as a small battery-powered light that I could turn on

with the flick of a switch. He had nothing more than the air that was inside his barrel and some extra air forced in with a bicycle pump. I had the whole filter system, as well as the oxygen tank. Once he was locked in he was by himself, no way to communicate with anybody. I was alone, but I wasn't isolated. I had a two-way radio. I could talk to Timmy and Boomer for at least part of the time—at least until I was underwater. If I was caught underneath I couldn't talk to them. It didn't really matter though. If I was trapped in the spin cycle beneath the Falls there was nothing for them to do anyway.

"It's the best thing we can build," Boomer said. "It's as perfect as I can figure."

I let out a sigh of relief. "It's good to know it's going to make it."

"I didn't say that," Boomer said. "If it goes over the wrong place or the wrong way, there ain't nothing perfect enough to stop it from getting smashed to pieces."

"You can't scare me," I said.

"You got nothing to be scared of from me," Boomer said. "It's the river that could kill you. I'm trying my best to keep you from dying, but you gotta know there's no guarantees."

"I know that," I said. "But do you *think* it'll work?"

"If I didn't, I wouldn't be letting you try."

"Have you figured out where we're going to put it in?" I asked.

He nodded his head. "Come on, I'll show you."

Boomer's car was parked in the driveway. I climbed in as he started the engine. He put it into gear and began to back up before I'd even put on my seat belt—and I really wanted to put on my seat belt. I'd driven with Boomer enough to know that he treated things like traffic lights and stop signs as suggestions. He would have lost his licence a long time ago if he hadn't known all the cops in town. Twice I'd been with him when he was stopped. A third time the cop had recognized Boomer and just waved him on before he came to a stop.

Boomer backed out of the driveway, knocking over a garbage can at the curb, and then squealed away down the street. He slowed down at the stop sign, glanced both ways, and then rolled through the intersection.

"That sign means stop, you know," I said.

"I slowed down, so what are you complaining about?"

"I prefer to stay alive, if you don't mind."

"You're going over the Falls and you're worried about my driving?"

"I'm not sure which is more dangerous."

"My driving is nothing. If you're getting cold feet maybe somebody else should go over," he said.

"You?" I questioned.

"I could be the oldest man to ever go over the Falls."

"You're joking, right?"

"Not joking about *thinking* about it. But doing it is a different thing. It's your barrel, your plan, your day, and I'm just along to help you."

"I'm just so glad you are helping. I don't know what would have happened without you."

"Probably death is what would have happened is my guess. But let's not talk about that. You still thinking in two days?"

"It's going to be ready. There's no point in waiting, is there?"

"Waiting wouldn't be bad. Might even be better."

Boomer came up to a red light, slowed down, and hung a right turn, the tires squealing in an attempt to hold the road.

"Why would it be better to wait?" I asked.

"It's like the old saying: *Patience is a virtue.*"

"I know another old saying: *He who hesitates is lost,*" I said in reply.

"Lost, but alive."

Boomer pulled the car over to the side and bounced two wheels up onto the sidewalk.

"Nice parking."

"Nice enough."

We got out of the car and walked toward the river. There were very few people along the path. They were all way downstream, at the Falls themselves, or looking down into the gorge.

"So where do you think we should put it in?"
I asked.

"Up there," he said, pointing slightly downriver.
"I think the truck should come right through here. You
got a truck, right?"

"One of my friends' big brother reserved it for us.
He's going to be the driver."

"Does he know what you're doing?"

"No. He thinks we're just moving some furniture. I thought it was better to tell as few people as
possible."

"Smart. And when he finds out what you're really
doing?"

"He'll be okay. He's used to doing things that aren't
exactly legal."

Boomer walked along the path and I followed
closely behind.

"He'll back it right up here, getting as close to the
railing as possible. Then the barrel has to be lifted out
and over."

"How many people do you think that'll take?" I
asked.

"At least ten. Can you get that many?"

"If I break open a two-four I can get more than
that. We get friends over but we won't tell them what
we're doing until they get there."

"They just have to hoist it over the railing. Once it
starts to roll down the slope nothing is going to stop it."

I pictured it rolling down the slope and splashing into the river. I could see it happening, although my view was going to be a lot different from the inside, spinning and spinning around.

"Munday put his barrel in just over there," Boomer said, pointing slightly upriver.

"Over there? How did they get the barrel over that railing? It's really high there."

"It's really high *now*. They put in higher railings to stop him from doing it again." Boomer laughed. "Like a railing is gonna stop Dave Munday. If he wanted to try it again he'd do it . . . and I'm not betting against him making a third trip over the Falls."

"So this is the spot, right?" I asked, needing reassurance.

"The current will take you straight out and into the centre, away from the rocks at the bottom."

"Then . . . then you think it'll work?"

"I think you've built a good barrel and made a good plan," Boomer said. "You've increased the odds."

"Enough to make it?"

"That's something I can't say. That's between you, the river, and God."

Boomer turned and walked away. I didn't follow. I leaned against the railing, looking out.

CHAPTER TWENTY-SEVEN

I PUSHED MY FOOD around the plate. I just wasn't hungry.

"Okay, so what's her name?"

I looked up at my mother. "What's whose name?"

"The girl that has you so distracted. You think I haven't noticed how you've been the last few weeks? Hardly eating, trouble sleeping, not paying attention when I talk to you. So, what's her name?"

What was I supposed to say—that there was no girl, that I was distracted because I was going to go over Niagara Falls in a barrel in the morning?

"Well?"

"Um . . . her name is . . . Amber."

My mother started to laugh.

"What's so funny?" I asked.

"It's just that if you'd been a girl instead of a boy that was going to be your name."

"I was going to be an Amber?" I questioned.

"That or Crystal. So, is she as pretty as her name?"

I pictured the barrel, all painted up in red and white. "Yeah, she's beautiful."

"When are you going to bring her around to the house?"

"She doesn't like to go out much." Actually, she just stayed there on blocks in the garage.

"Sounds like she's shy. I like that in a girl. Some of the girls today seem downright aggressive. Where did you meet her?"

"Just around."

"Well, if this gets any more serious I'd like to meet her. You could bring her around for supper."

"Sure, I could do that."

"Good. You're going to make some lucky girl a great husband someday."

"I'm only fifteen! I'm not about to get married!" I protested.

"Not now. That's why I said *someday*. A long time from now. It's just that I know that with any relation-ship there's potential for pain and heartache. I've never seen you so distracted, so she must be impor-tant to you. A broken heart is a lot more painful than any of those broken bones you've had."

"Nobody's going to break my heart," I protested. Broken bones were more of a worry right now.

"I hope you're wrong."

That sure wasn't what I'd expected. "You *want* somebody to break my heart?"

"The only people who don't get hurt are those who don't take risks. They call it *falling* in love because you lose control . . . you're falling . . . and when you fall sometimes you get hurt."

She had no idea how true those words were.

My mother got up from the table, circled around, and gave me a big hug around my shoulders. I buried my head into her. It felt so good. She released her grip so she was now facing me.

"I wish I could protect you from all the pain in life, but I can't. No more than I could protect myself. Of course, the only thing worse than feeling that pain yourself is watching somebody you love go through it."

I knew that first-hand. I'd seen my mother go through some bad times and bad relationships.

"The secret is to not let the fear of hurt stop you from taking the risk. Do you remember a conversation we had at the beginning of the summer, when you asked me if you were a loser?"

"Yeah . . . I guess . . . sort of." I was lying. I remembered it very well.

"I've thought about it a lot," she said. "I shouldn't have said what I said."

"That it was still too early to say if I was a loser."

"I thought you only *sort of* remembered."

"You mentioning it brought it back. It's no big deal."

"It is. I shouldn't have said that."

"Shouldn't have said it because you didn't want to hurt my feelings?"

"Shouldn't have said it because I was wrong. After I said it, I starting thinking about what makes people winners or losers. And then I remembered something my father used to say to me. He told me that a person is only a loser when they stop trying to win."

"I'm not a quitter," I said.

"I know you're not. You're one of the most determined people I know, so in answer to that question you asked me, no, you're not a loser. You're a winner."

"Thanks . . . I guess."

"Nobody in the whole history of the world has had everything go right. Nobody lives a perfect life. The winners aren't those who never fall down, but those who get back up after they fall and keep going. I know I haven't given you the easiest life."

"It could have been worse."

"It could have been better. A lot better. You've had more than your fair share of knocks. But you've never stayed down. Promise me you'll keep getting back up."

"I promise," I said, although there was one fall—one fall that was going to take place tomorrow—that I had no control over.

"Now, I'd better get to work or I'll be late." She stood up, grabbed her purse, and started for the back door.

"Mom?" I called out, and she stopped and turned. "Do you think I could sleep at Timmy's tonight? You're not going to be in until late anyway." We were going to be up and in the truck before four in the morning so that the barrel would be in the water before six.

"Does this, by any chance, involve a girl named Amber?"

"No. I promise you, there isn't going to be any Amber tonight. Timmy and me are just going to hang around, watch a movie or two, maybe go on the Internet."

She didn't answer right away. "So if I was to call Timmy's house around midnight you'd be there, right?"

"You could call any time and we'd be there."

"Okay. You and Timmy enjoy the movies. When are you heading over?"

"Timmy's going to pick me up and we're going to our meeting."

"That's right, that's tonight. I'm so pleased you boys enjoy those meetings."

"I don't think 'enjoy' is the word I'd use . . . but we go. Isn't that enough?"

"More than enough."

She came back across the room and gave me a kiss on the top of my head. I reached up and wrapped my arms around her.

"I love you, Mom."

"That's so nice to hear. I love you, Jay. We don't say that enough."

I couldn't help wondering—would this be the last time I ever said it to her? Would this be the last time I ever hugged her? Would this be the last time I ever saw her?

"THERE'S A DIFFERENCE between 'explanation' and 'excuse,'" Mrs. Bayliss said.

"I'm not following you," Timmy answered.

"Me neither," said one of the girls. She was new to the group—I didn't know her name, but Amber or Crystal was probably a good guess.

"It's a fact that people who have an alcoholic parent are more likely to be alcoholics," Mrs. Bayliss explained.

"It's in the genes," Desiree said.

"Probably there is a genetic component, but it also might be learned behaviour. If your parents like ice cream and you see them eat ice cream all the time, it's more likely you're going to like ice cream too."

"That makes sense," Timmy agreed.

"But which do you think it is?" somebody asked.

"I think it's both," Mrs. Bayliss said. "But neither is an excuse."

"I still don't get that part," Timmy said.

"I do," I said.

"Can you explain it to me?" Timmy asked.

"It means that whether it's something you learn or something you inherit, it's still your choice if you're going to drink." I turned to Mrs. Bayliss. "Right?"

"I couldn't have said it better myself. Too often people use what happens to them as an excuse. They say things like 'I couldn't help being an alcoholic because my parents are alcoholics' . . . 'I can't help myself' . . . 'There was nothing I could do' . . . 'It wasn't my fault.'"

"That's a lot of crap," I said.

"I agree, but people are always making excuses for things. It's easier to make an excuse than find an answer. One of the things that frustrates me the most as a teacher is seeing kids who could make it, but never do. They waste their lives because it's easier to have an excuse to fail than to buckle down and succeed."

I got the feeling she was directing that comment to me. Maybe she was directing it to all of us.

"This is our last meeting together this summer," Mrs. Bayliss said.

"But we are going to be on again next week, right?" Desiree asked.

"We'll be meeting, but not all of us will be here."

"Why not?" Timmy asked.

"I'm going away to university," Jason said.

"And I'm off to college," Chantel added.

"I didn't know you two were going away," Timmy said.

"You're both going to be missed. Missed, but not forgotten," Mrs. Bayliss told them. Then she said, to the whole group, "I just wanted to tell you, before we break for the evening, that it's been a pleasure to work with all of you."

People voiced agreement. It actually hadn't been that bad at all.

"I was thinking that I'd like to adjourn the meeting early tonight. I'm inviting all of you to come downstairs to the pizza parlour for food and drinks . . . my treat."

We all trooped downstairs. Everyone was in kind of a party mood, but I couldn't help thinking about the condemned prisoner's last meal. I guess pizza was what I'd have chosen if I knew for sure the end was near.

Mrs. Bayliss settled into the seat beside me. "You and Timmy have been good additions to the group. You've really made a contribution."

"Thanks."

"Now I'm hoping you'll make just as big a contribution starting next Tuesday, first day of school."

"I'll be there."

"I'd like all of you to be there," she said. "I'd be interested to see what you could do if you really tried your hardest. It's not just Chantel and Jason who can go away to school. Have you given any more thought to being an engineer?"

"I think about a lot of things."

"Keep thinking about that one. Once school starts I'll get information for you about which universities might be best, scholarship opportunities, student loans." She paused. "That is, if you'd like me to do that."

"I'd like that. Could you also look up stuff about becoming a pilot?"

"You want to become a pilot?"

"Not me. Timmy."

She nodded. "I'll find out everything I can. Enjoy your pizza and order another beer . . . another root beer."

IT WAS WEIRD going back to Timmy's that night, sitting around watching TV as if nothing was going to happen, and knowing that only a few hours stood between me and what I was about to do.

It wasn't like I didn't believe Boomer when he said I could die. I knew it in my head and I felt it in my gut, but I knew there was nothing that I could do to stop it. It was like I'd set off the timer on a bomb and it was ticking away and I was powerless to stop it. No, that wasn't right. You could always cut the wires . . . that's what they did on TV shows. They just cut the wires and the ticking stopped.

This was more like being caught up in a current. Once you were in the middle of the river there was no going back. I was sitting in Timmy's living room but I was already out there. There was no stopping, no going back, no matter how much I struggled. All I could do now was hope for the best.

If it worked, I'd be stupid rich, and Timmy would be doing okay as well. We'd both have enough money to do whatever we wanted . . . whatever that was. But really, I wasn't sure how much of this had anything to do with the money. It had more to do with proving something. Or maybe disproving some other things. I didn't really know which parts of me were from my father, or my grandfather, or even my great-grandfather. I didn't know if I was trying to show how brave I was, or that I was a riverman, or maybe simply that I wasn't a loser. Yeah, I'd show everybody that I was no loser.

I took another sip from the bottle of beer. Timmy had scrounged a six-pack. He said he'd "liberated" it from his father, who was passed out in front of the TV. A few beers were okay, but I wouldn't have drunk more, even if we'd had them. I needed to face up to what I was about to do stone-cold sober. But a couple of beers might just help me get to sleep. Sleep . . . that seemed as impossible as anything I'd ever imagined.

CHAPTER TWENTY-EIGHT

"ARE YOU ASLEEP?" Timmy asked, his voice whispering out of the darkness.

"No."

"I don't think I slept at all."

"Me neither," I replied.

"Maybe we should just get up. What time is it?"

"Quarter to four. We might as well. The truck will be here soon."

We'd only told the guys part of the truth. Instead of offering them some beer we'd told them that we were doing something illegal. They probably thought they were going to rip something off—something big, since we needed a truck. It was amazing how easy it was to recruit people to commit a crime. That really said something about the type of people we hung around with.

I pulled myself up and sat on the edge of the bed. I saw the darkened image of Timmy sit up too. He'd slept on the floor because he said it was more important that I sleep well than him. Obviously it hadn't helped either of us.

Timmy worked his way across the room and flicked on a little light that sat on a table in the corner. I shielded my eyes.

"What do you want for breakfast?" he asked.

"I don't know if I should have anything. It's probably better if my stomach is empty."

"You have to have something. At least a coffee and some cereal. You're not going over till after six."

I followed Timmy out of his bedroom. As we cut across the living room I caught sight of his father, still asleep in his chair, the TV still glowing. The coffee table was crowded with empty beer bottles and an overflowing ashtray, and the air was heavy with a pungent combination of alcohol and smoke. I tiptoed past him.

Timmy was already in the kitchen, opening and closing drawers.

"Shouldn't you be more quiet?" I asked.

"Don't worry," Timmy said. "Once he's passed out nothing can wake him. If the alcohol doesn't kill him then he's going to pass out with a cigarette in his hand and set himself on fire. Just so you know, we have cereal," he said, holding up a box of Cheerios, "but we don't have any milk . . . well, at least any milk that isn't slightly green . . . green is not a good colour for milk."

"I'll just have the cereal," I said, taking the box from him.

Timmy put on the coffee while I reached in and grabbed a fistful of cereal. It was slightly stale, but it didn't really matter. And it was also probably a good thing that there wasn't any milk. Dry cereal would sit in my stomach better. There was no telling how bad the ride was going to be, and the last thing I wanted to do was throw up inside the barrel.

I turned when I heard the sound of an engine.

"That's probably the truck," Timmy said.

I hurried to the back door, opened it up, and peered outside. I couldn't see the source of the sound. Then I saw a little light come on inside a car parked on the road. It was Boomer's car! Boomer got out and started up the driveway.

"Good morning," he called out as he got closer.

"What are you doing here?" He wasn't supposed to be part of this. He was going to be down below on the river to pull me out, but he'd already said he couldn't help put me into the river.

"Wouldn't 'good morning' be a more friendly reply?" he asked.

"Yeah . . . sure. Good morning. Why are you here?" I was afraid he was going to try to talk me out of it.

"I'm here to make sure everything goes the way it's supposed to. Make sure the last-minute details go right."

"But what about pulling me out?"

"I'll be there, too. I'll leave before they put you in the water. Don't worry, I'll give myself enough time to get down below."

"Okay . . . good."

"Where's the truck?"

"It should be here any minute."

Almost on cue, two bright lights turned in and the big panel truck bumped up the driveway. I should have been relieved—I had been worried that they wouldn't show up. Instead I felt my stomach tighten into a fist. We were one step closer.

"I'll talk to the guys," Timmy said. "You go and get the barrel ready for loading."

"Do you think they're going to be okay with this?" I asked.

"Are you kidding? What kid who grew up in the Falls wouldn't want to be part of this?"

THE TRUCK BUMPED and rolled and I struggled to stay on my feet. I was standing in the back, holding on to the side of the barrel with one hand and the side of the truck with the other as we were jostled around. Boomer sat on the bench, staring into space. He hadn't spoken since before the barrel had been loaded into the truck. I needed him to say something.

"Do you think we can get past the Parks staff to put it into the river?" I asked.

"You mean put *you* in the river."

"Well, yeah. Me in the barrel."

"It's time for you to get into the barrel," Boomer said as he stood up. He kept one hand on the side of the truck to steady himself as he shuffled along.

"Now?" I looked at my watch. "It's still thirty-five minutes before we put the barrel—me—into the river."

"I want to make sure everything works right before I leave. It'll take me at least fifteen minutes to get to the same spot it'll take you fifteen seconds to reach."

"Do you really think it could only take fifteen seconds?"

"Fifteen seconds. Fifteen minutes. Fifteen hours. Once you get into the river it's up to God."

"I didn't think you believed in God," I said.

"I don't, but I don't have to. It's not me going over the Falls. Now get in."

I didn't move. My legs suddenly felt dead.

Boomer opened up the hatch. "Come on, hurry up."

I bumped into the side of the truck. I grabbed the top of the hatch then, and swung my legs up, smacking my left knee in the process, and slipped into the barrel.

I suddenly felt very hot. How could the air in the barrel be so much hotter than it was in the back of the truck? But it wasn't . . . it was me. My whole body felt flushed. I was radiating heat. My heart was pumping so hard I could almost hear it beating.

"Hurry up and get into your harness," Boomer said.

I fumbled around for the straps, my hands shaking and sweating. What had been so easy before was now a struggle. I managed to do up the buckles holding my legs in place, and moved up to the next set that would hold my midsection.

"Get 'em tight," Boomer ordered. "Too loose and they won't do you any good."

I pulled the strap tight, feeling it pressing, almost digging into my abdomen.

"Can you reach your oxygen tank?"

I spun partway around and put a hand on the nozzle. "I can reach."

"You sure the tank is fully charged . . . that it's full of oxygen?" Boomer asked.

"Why wouldn't it be?" I asked in reply. "Timmy just got it from the scuba store and—"

"Have *you* checked it?" Boomer asked, cutting me off.

"No," I admitted. I didn't even know how to check.

"So you're trusting that some joker in the scuba store—some joker you've never even met—isn't shortchanging you. How do you know the tank is completely full? Maybe you don't have thirty minutes. Maybe there's only twenty minutes of air. Maybe it's only half full and there's fifteen minutes. Maybe it's empty."

My heart started pounding even harder. I didn't know what to say.

"Do you know?" he snapped. "Well, do you?"

I shook my head.

"Well, *I* know. I checked the pressure. It's fully charged."

"Why didn't you just tell me?" I asked angrily.

"Why didn't you just ask me?" he snapped back. "You want my help or what?"

"Yeah . . . of course . . . it's just that you got me all worried."

"If you weren't really worried before this then you just don't understand nothing that's going on, son. Now, you gotta remember that thirty minutes' worth of air is just my guess. If you breathe really relaxed it could last over forty minutes. Panic and it will be gone in less than twenty."

"I'm not going to panic."

Boomer scowled. "If you need to use that tank it's because you're caught behind the Falls, being cycled around and around, trapped in the undertow. Do you have any idea what that would be like?"

I shook my head. "No . . . what would it be like?" I asked, although I almost didn't want to know.

"I don't know either. Nobody knows. The only people who ever got caught never lived to tell of it."

A visible shudder ran through my entire body.

"Do up the last straps so I can close the hatch."

"We don't have to close it yet, do we?"

"We don't have to keep it closed but we have to test it one more time."

Quickly I worked to do up the last part of the harness. I was now completely suspended, hanging there in the little hammock-type arrangement. I rocked back and forth, swaying slightly, but secure, away from all sides of the barrel.

Without warning the hatch slammed shut and I jerked in my harness. It was suddenly dark—or at least darker. My eyes tried to adjust to the limited light coming in through the porthole on the hatch. I reached up and switched on the little battery-powered lamp that was attached to the ceiling of the chamber. It filled the barrel with light. That was better . . . or should I turn it off? I didn't want to waste the batteries in case I needed them if I was trapped. Then again, it didn't matter. If I was caught in the undertow my air would give out long before the batteries would.

It was eerily quiet. The sounds of the road and the truck were so muffled that I could barely hear them at all. What I heard was the echoing of my breath. And I had the strangest thought: if you were buried alive, is that what it would sound like inside your coffin?

I took a deep breath and held it. Would I be able to relax if I needed to? I didn't know. I *couldn't* know until it happened. Then I heard the sound of Boomer tightening the screws down to hold the hatch in place. Each turn meant the hatch was getting tighter, more secure, safer . . . and I was getting more deeply trapped inside. My whole body, from my toes to my fingertips, began to sweat. I was now helpless. I was locked inside, unable to control the barrel rolling down the slope and into the river and surging toward the Falls and then over the edge and dropping and— There were no more sounds. The hatch was tightened down. Now he could open it up and I could breathe some fresh air. In a few seconds now he'd start unscrewing it. There was silence. Why wasn't he opening it? What was wrong? Boomer was going to open it up again, wasn't he? This was just a test, right? He wasn't just going to let me stay inside until I got pushed into the river, was he? I tried to replay the conversation we'd had when I climbed inside. He had said this was just a test, that it didn't have to stay sealed . . . that was what he'd said, wasn't it?

Desperately I arched my neck so I could see out through the tiny porthole. I hoped to see something—a little glimpse of Boomer—anything. All I could see was the back panel door of the truck. The truck . . . we weren't moving anymore. We'd arrived at the wall, and maybe they didn't have time to unseal me and seal me back up again. I closed my eyes and brought my hands together and started to pray. I didn't know if there really was a God.

I didn't know if He even listened to people's prayers. I didn't know if I even deserved to have Him listen to mine.

Dear God . . . it's me . . . Jay . . . Jayson Hunter. Could I . . . could I . . . could I have one more breath of air . . . please could they open the hatch and let me——?

I heard the screws again and saw Boomer through the hatch. He was opening it up!

Thank you . . . thank you . . . and . . . and . . . amen.

I tried to slow down my breathing, regain my composure. I turned off the light and closed my eyes to try to block out the dark—to try to block out everything. In only a few seconds the hatch would open . . . only to be closed up again in a few minutes . . . a dozen minutes . . . maybe half an hour. The timing would depend upon the patrols by the park rangers and the police. But I'd been over the timing. There was plenty of time between the patrols so there wasn't going to be any problem.

Then I had the strangest thought. Maybe it would be better if we *did* get caught and—— The hatch popped open. Cool air and sounds from the truck's engine flooded into the barrel.

"So?" Boomer asked.

"I'm okay," I said. My voice sounded different . . . strained ... like it wasn't even mine.

"Do you feel it yet?" Boomer asked.

"Feel what?"

"That buzz in the back of your head you get from doing something risky."

I didn't feel anything. My head—my whole body—just felt numb.

"I'm feeling it, and I'm not even in the barrel," Boomer said. "Same high any addict gets when he's getting his fix. So, are you feeling it?"

"Um . . . no . . . not yet."

"We're coming up to the stop where I'm gonna be leaving."

"Already?"

"I told you, I have to get down below and be ready to get you out." He paused. "You sure you're okay?"

I nodded my head.

"You know, you don't have to do this."

"What?"

"You don't have to do this," Boomer repeated. "You can climb out right now and nobody will think any less of you."

"Of course they will!" I exclaimed. "I can't just walk away. Not after all this work. Not after everything we've done . . . all the time and money that has been invested."

"You could walk away, right now."

"What would everybody say?"

"Do you really care what everybody would say?"

"Well . . . what about Timmy? What would he think?"

"He'd think you were doing the right thing. I know that. He doesn't want you to go . . . he told me."

My head was suddenly spinning around. I didn't know what to think, what to say.

"Why are you doing it?" Boomer asked. "Why are you going over the Falls? Is it for the thrill?"

"Not the thrill," I said. "For the money, I guess. To make it big. You know how much money this would be worth. It's my way out."

"Out of what?"

"Out of here. Out of the Falls."

"What's so bad about being here?"

"You wouldn't understand."

"Why wouldn't I?"

"It's just that you *like* living here. You left and you came back," I said.

"So did you. You and your mother lived other places before you came back here," Boomer said.

"That wasn't my choice. If I stay here it's like . . . like . . . I'll never be anything."

"And you want to be more. You want to be an engineer, right?"

"I want to be *something*."

"You'd be a good engineer. This is a beautiful piece of work," he said, putting a hand against the barrel.

"Good enough to make it over the Falls?"

"As good as anything I've seen."

"Then maybe I have to try."

"That's not what I'm saying. You don't have to try anything. If you do, you do, but do it for the right reasons. You want out of here, you want to become an engineer, I can help."

"How can you help?" I asked.

"I've got money," Boomer said.

"It'll cost a fortune. Besides, I can't just let you give me money," I said.

"I'm not talking about *giving* you anything. I'm talking about you working for it. More hours during the school year and full-time every summer. Not to mention that I just might make you an offer for the barrel. You were right when you said it would make a pretty fine display in the museum."

"I can't let you do that either. I know there's not enough money coming in for that. I know the museum doesn't make that much."

"The museum is just my hobby. I got lots of money. Who do you think owns the parking lot *beside* the museum?" Boomer asked. "Bought that twenty years ago. And I'm a partial owner of a couple of restaurants in town—sort of an investor. And then there's the houses. I own five houses that I rent out."

"I didn't know."

"That's because I don't talk about it. Not everybody who lives here is a loser, you know."

"I didn't mean that . . . I didn't mean you were a loser."

"The Falls is like every other place. It's got good and bad, winners and losers—in things and people. A man isn't defined by *where* he lives, but by *how* he lives."

The truck still wasn't moving—the engine was silent. Suddenly the back door of the truck was flung open and Timmy and the driver were standing there, looking up.

"We're here at the parking lot," Timmy said.

"We need some more time," Boomer said.

"But if we don't go now we'll have to wait until—"

"We need more time!" Boomer yelled. "Now close the door and leave us alone!"

Timmy looked shocked, but he listened.

"What about Timmy?" I asked. "I can't leave him behind. He has a dream too."

"Nobody's asking you to. I'll help him the same way I'm gonna help you. I'll help him chase down his dreams. What does he want to be?"

"A pilot."

"Pilot!" Boomer exclaimed. "I'll help him get there . . . although there's no way I'm ever gonna climb into any plane that he's flying. Well . . . what do you think?"

I didn't answer. I didn't know if I had the strength to climb out of the barrel.

"Sometimes the bravest thing somebody can do is simply say no. Are you brave enough to walk away?"

I shook my head. "I don't know."

"I think I do. Let's just call it quits for today," Boomer said. "You don't have to close the door forever, just for today. I'll make you a deal. I'll keep the barrel right there in the museum. You work and keep an eye on it. Five years from now, if you decide you want to go over the Falls, then it's yours again."

"Really?"

"For sure . . . unless of course I decide to use it myself."

"What?"

Boomer started chuckling. "Remember what I said—I could get into the record books as the oldest man to go over the Falls."

"You wouldn't do it, really, would you?"

He shook his head. "Can't risk it. Got things I have to take care of. Somebody's gotta keep an eye on you and Timmy. Now get yourself out of there!"

I undid the straps holding me in. I started to climb out and Boomer gave me a hand. I slipped out, feeling like the weight of the world had been lifted off my shoulders.

"You know, Jay, if you'd done it—if you'd gone over the Falls—you probably would have made it," Boomer said.

"I know," I said. "Probably. But this way, I *know* I'm going to make it."